THE ELVEN STONES: FAMILY

P. A. WILSON

Free ebook

Claim your copy of Obstacles of Magic when you use the QR code to sign up for my newsletter and learn more about Madeline's history with magic.

Chapter 1

Willowvine stuffed her black scarf into her backpack. This job wasn't likely to go wrong, but she didn't want to be recognized, and the scarf would cover everything that revealed she was an elf. The guild defined legal a little differently from the way the law did. Even so, if she got caught it wouldn't be sure that she'd walk free.

"Why does the guild always send us on these kinds of jobs?" she asked Springheart.

Looking over, she saw him chuckling as he prepared his own pack. In the five years they'd been working as a team for the courier's guild, they'd retrieved a lot of stolen items. The guild was always clear that the items had already been stolen, so taking them back wasn't a crime. Willowvine figured if they were such a special team, maybe they should get more of a fee. When they had more savings, she'd be able to convince Springheart to start their own guild, one that was actually friendly to elves rather than indifferent at best.

Springheart picked up his cloak before he answered. He gave her that look. The one that said she should know the answer, but when she didn't speak, he shrugged and said,

"Because we are the best at it. We get in and out fast and quiet. It helps to have your ability to know if anyone is lurking."

Willowvine smiled and shrugged the pack on. "Like we did at the gate between worlds? Saving all of Cartref and then being exiled without so much as a thank you."

"I don't know why you expected any different." Springheart didn't meet her eyes. He paid attention to getting his cloak folded just right.

Willowvine knew he was hiding his own disappointment. Just because he didn't talk about it didn't mean he agreed with the way the elves treated orphans. She knew that people didn't lose their prejudices easily. "I guess it's not that much different from how they treated the scree who helped us. He was different too. Although, I guess, it's been a while since any scree acted on a blood feud, maybe they are losing their warrior culture."

A lot of the beings had changed in the last five years. It was like everyone sensed that the only danger of war was from internal pressure. Without the threat of an invasion, it was possible to live peacefully.

It was time to go and she didn't want to be overheard talking about her plans in the street. There would be people around, there always were, and she didn't want to start an argument if Springheart didn't agree. She took one last look. Their room was tidy. The two beds always made because Springheart believed that keeping their home neat would keep their minds clear. She didn't care. The room was small enough that it didn't take much to deal with. And it meant the landlady stayed out of their business.

They walked to the job side by side. Willowvine waited for a good time to broach the subject of her plans. It was harder than she thought. Maybe she should just tell him despite being in a public place. "I've been thinking." Then she stalled. Springheart didn't really like change, and this was a big one.

He glanced over at her, but didn't say anything.

"About our next jobs." She hoped that he would ask. It was too hard to just speak, and she couldn't just blurt it out. They arrived at the job before she could think of a way to say what she needed to say.

The house was dark as promised. Their job was to retrieve a ledger that the tenant had stolen from a rival. Willowvine closed her eyes while Springheart pulled out the ropes they'd use to scale the walls. Her magic wasn't warning her that anyone was thinking about any danger, or that anyone was particularly alert, so it was probably safe. She knew Springheart would want it that way. He liked safe jobs. She preferred a little risk to make things fun.

"It's all clear," she whispered. "After, I don't want to just go back to our room." She thought maybe a mug of beer would help her bring the subject up again.

"You want to talk about our next jobs," Springheart said. "Sure, we can talk about anything when this one is done."

She nodded and took the rope he'd coiled to loop over her shoulder. There was a wall to climb and a yard to cross. And then a house wall to climb before she reached the window. For the first time, she was going on her own. It would be her going to the room where the ledger was hidden according to a servant they'd bribed. This was the part that always made her tense, the time when everything could go wrong. The point where they didn't know if the information was good, or if someone was betraying them.

Knowing that Springheart wouldn't be there to cover her back made it worse. Her sense for peril had never let them down before. She was just waiting for the day when it did. She knew that if they moved fast, they would be fine, but Springheart was always worried about being safe. This time he wouldn't be there to do that.

Springheart looked up at the wall and nodded. She took a

few steps back and ran toward the wall to gain enough momentum to leap to the top. This was what he'd meant when he'd said they were the best at it. Elves were able to get into places that other species found impossible.

They went over the wall together and landed silently on the grass that surrounded the house. There was no other security, but there was still a possibility of someone seeing them. Springheart tapped her shoulder and they ran to the house, coming to a stop in the shadows of the overhang. Looking up, she saw that the house was going to be a lot easier than the wall. There were trellises and ledges within easy reach.

Willowvine knew that Springheart kept watch for her as she scaled to the third-floor window. It wasn't the same as him being there beside her, but it was a comfort.

Perching on the ledge, she looked into the room. The curtains were open. So far, their source was coming through. Peeking inside, she saw a desk, a set of straight-backed chairs, and a bookshelf. The only light was what filtered in through the window, more than sufficient for elven eyes.

A quick glance at Springheart before she started to open the window showed him scanning the yard, trusting that she would do her job. Sliding a metal tool from inside her jacket, Willowvine placed it between the window and the frame. A jiggle of the bar shifted the window and gave her hope that it would slide up without noise. She prised the window up slowly, using the tool to prop it open as soon as there was enough room for her to slip inside.

The ledger was supposed to be inside a desk drawer. If she could get the drawer open, then she'd take the ledger and join Springheart. If she couldn't, or anything went wrong, she'd drop something to get his attention and he'd climb up and help. She hated thinking through these details, but if she were successful, it would help boost her argument when she talked to him later about their future. A future where elven orphans were respected not ignored.

Willowvine moved to the desk. There were ten drawers. She ignored the center drawer; it was too shallow to hold the target. A tug at the others revealed that they were all locked. As much as she wanted this over with, Willowvine knew that she had to go slowly and leave no trace. Pulling picks out of her pocket, she started with the bottom drawers. They opened easily, but didn't contain the ledger. She kept picking locks until she found what she needed in the top right-hand drawer. As she pulled the ledger out a noise came from outside the room.

SPRINGHEART KEPT his focus on the surrounding yard. If anyone decided to take a late-night stroll on the grounds, they might get trapped. The best way to get this kind of job done was fast. The conditions were perfect. It was calm tonight. Their inside man had assured the guild that the owners would be away. The servants were in the house, but they wouldn't move from their common room.

Assurances were fine, but Springheart would trust the information when the job was done, and nothing would be able to go wrong.

A pebble dropped beside him. Willowvine was on her way down.

He glanced up from his survey of the grounds to see her perched on the edge of the windowsill, back to him, closing the window. Her hair glinted in the moonlight. She wasn't careful enough about the scarf. If people saw her without it there was no doubt that she was an elf. With the scarf, she could pass as a human child of eight or nine. Her real age of thirty or so, still young for an elf but not a child, was apparent as soon as anyone saw the silvery hair.

As he watched she twisted on her toes and looked down at

him. Then she stepped off the ledge, dropping to the second-floor sill as though it was a step on a deep staircase. Hardly landing before she left it to drop beside him.

"In a rush?" he asked as she stood from the crouch.

"There's someone there. Let's go." She tapped her chest as she spoke. The thud let him know she'd been successful.

He grabbed her arm as she moved to run across the lawn. "Let me check it out first."

He still couldn't get her to use caution. If someone was prowling around inside the house, they could easily be in the study, looking out the window, ready to raise the alarm.

When she nodded, he stepped quietly from shadow to shadow until he had a clear view of the window. No outline of a person showed in the glass. He crept back to her and nodded for Willowvine to run for the wall. When she was halfway across, he started his own escape; every second he was in open sight he felt an arrow aimed at his back. They vaulted the wall, coming to rest in its shadow.

He made her stay in place for long enough to catch their breath and to ensure no alarm sounded. Springheart used the time to calm his anger. They never left a job in this kind of hurry unless something was wrong. They never did anything wrong, otherwise they would not be the best in the guild. When they were together, Willowvine followed his guidance. Tonight, she had been on her own. He hadn't liked the idea, but he knew that she was champing to become his equal, and she was in most respects. She was just too much of a risk taker to be truly safe on her own.

The biggest problem he had in keeping her safe was that while she was old enough to be expert at what they did, she was still too young to understand the repercussions of her actions.

Breathing under control, Springheart nudged her. "I'll take

the ledger. We don't want it falling out of your shirt in the middle of the street."

Letting go of the grip she had around her chest to hold the ledger inside her shirt, she wiggled and let the book slide onto her lap. They stored it in the bag, safe until it was delivered to the guildhall.

"There was someone in the house," she said as they stood and began the short walk to the guildhall. "Someone was outside the study."

"So, you decided to just run?" Springheart knew that she wouldn't have run if there was a chance she'd been seen. Hiding was a much better strategy.

She sighed and jabbed him with her elbow. "Yeah, I thought it was best to lead them to you." When he didn't respond, she added, "No. Whoever it was didn't come into the room. And before you ask, I locked the drawer before I left."

Springheart smiled despite his worry. She was good at this, and soon she'd be able to go on solo jobs. It wasn't something he looked forward to. The relationship was a surprise to him. Both of them were orphans, something that got you exiled from the elven society, and when they had started working together, after helping to save the world from invasion, he'd expected them to be like brother and sister. It never got there. They were partners almost from the moment they left Madeline's house.

"Did you see that?" Willowvine's voice was low, but alertness sharpened it.

Springheart had seen the shadow that slipped from a doorway to follow them. "Can you sense anything?" Her ability to sense auras had saved their reputations too many times to count.

She took his arm, letting him lead her while her focus was on her magic. It took only a few steps before she was able to answer. "Nothing strong, and it's a bit muddled. There's a feeling of irritation, I guess. Nothing overtly dangerous."

If Willowvine hadn't sensed danger in the spirit of whoever was following, then it could just be someone from the guild. They occasionally sent backup without letting couriers know. Well, it was more like checkup than backup.

"You wanted to talk about something?" If their shadow was from the guild, they could relax, if not, conversation would make them seem like they were not paying attention.

"I'm not sure it's a topic for the street." Willowvine stopped, bent, and fiddled with her bootlaces. She was checking their tail. "He's gone."

"Then you can tell me what you wanted to talk about," Springheart said, knowing that if they didn't get the topic out in the open, she'd start the conversation when he was trying to sleep.

"Are you still okay taking contracts from the guild? Ones we really have no choice but to take?"

This wasn't a new conversation. "If we go freelance, how will we get contracts?"

"I've been thinking about that," she said. "We could talk to previous clients. We could ask them for referrals. Lots of people ask for us. Maybe when we aren't available at the guild, they'll come looking for us."

He tried to look at it with a fresh point of view. He didn't like the fact that the guild told them what to do, but he also knew how hard it was for elves to get work. No matter the reputation they had, people liked to make deals with people who were like them. The guild had representation from all species that might want work done.

All except elves. Elves rarely had a need for the guild's services. When they did, the elves used intermediaries, and even then, they wouldn't want two orphans.

Chapter 2

Vitenkar paced the barracks. He'd managed to gather enough of an army to begin his plans. Taking Cartref for the scree was not going to be an easy campaign. Making the elves extinct would only be the first small victory.

He ordered the soldiers to silence. They obeyed slowly. He would make them regret that. Punish a few and the others would give him more respect, especially if he acted harshly. He might be a merchant, but he still braided the bones of his enemies in his hair. Just because the bones came in a box with the names carved on them, they were no less impressive than if he had ended the life himself.

"You have come to join the glorious battle for this world," he said.

No one cheered.

These were not the best warriors, they were sullen and preferred gaming to training, but he would get them into shape quickly. He would have them eager to do battle soon enough.

He looked out over the group. There were almost fifty scree in the room. They lounged on the beds, or sat in groups huddled around interrupted dice games, or half-drunk bottles of cheap liquor. Few of them had many bones threaded into their braids. New to battle they had yet to gain trophies.

"We have the prize we need to start our campaign," he roared the words as though it was a hard-won victory.

A few of his followers applauded, but most looked like they wanted him to finish so they could return to their games, bottles, or sleep. He couldn't manage them all, the only option was to elevate one or two of them to be his lieutenants, charge them with morale, and punish them if the troops didn't respond as expected.

He looked around for the ones who had applauded. Two of them were watching him with what might be interest. "You, and you," he said, pointing to them. "Meet me in the antechamber. The rest of you go back to your idleness. We will see action soon."

The two scree followed him from the barracks. At the bottom of the great stairs, Vitenkar motioned for them to stop. He strode to the storeroom and checked that the door was locked. The artifact was safely hidden and the door was secure.

"The antechamber," he ordered. The second floor was where he planned his campaign and where he slept. The meeting rooms on the first floor were small and he kept his business papers there. He didn't want his trading activities interrupted. Armies cost money and he couldn't risk losing the men he had, no matter how inferior.

The small antechamber to his bedroom was where he met important clients, and now where he would meet with the few people who would help him to achieve victory. The two scree he'd chosen led the way into the small room. It held a cabinet, where the best of the local wine and liquor were locked, a sofa, and a table large enough to seat six scree, or humans.

"Your names?" he asked as he unlocked the cabinet.

"Dintral, clan Leesot," the shorter one stated immediately.

Vitenkar wondered if he had chosen poorly when the taller

one looked him over before answering. "Ballian clan Druth. Why have you asked us here?"

It might be better to work with Ballian, Vitenkar thought. Blind loyalty wasn't always the most useful in a war. Vitenkar offered them wine, and indicated they should sit at the table. He pulled a roll of plans from the back of the cabinet and joined them.

"You know the story about the gate between worlds?" He waited until they nodded. The gate had been unknown to anyone but the elves until five years ago, when a woman had sealed it, saving the world from a violent and catastrophic invasion. "It seems all of Cartref is ready to live a future of peace and harmony."

"Not everyone," Ballian said. "Peace is boring. Look at your soldiers down there. That's the best of what's left of the scree warriors."

Vitenkar smiled. He had chosen well with Ballian. "Exactly. But they are still better warriors than any other race can bring to a battle. The elves have dismantled their armies and turned their energies to teaching and healing."

Dintral snickered. "There's no one left to fight."

Vitenkar glared at Dintral. "That isn't true. The scree are not willing to become traders and farmers. We are warriors."

"So, you want to fight the elves?" Dintral asked.

Vitenkar noticed that Ballian was keeping silent. The man was cunning. He would have to find a use for that. "The elves first."

"Like a tournament?" Dintral asked. "That would be fun. We could have prizes."

"No," Vitenkar shouted, slamming his hand on the table. "This is not a game. The scree will rule this world. The other beings will die or be enslaved."

"That's quite a goal." Ballian sat forward, eager to get

started. "Why the elves first? They are strong in battle and do not flinch from an army."

Vitenkar took a long sip of his wine. He did not want to be interrupted again. In the pause, he stared down both of his lieutenants, cowing them into listening. When he felt they were sufficiently attentive he started explaining. "The elves don't reproduce often. I have found a way to stop them from having any children at all. We need only cut down the existing villages. They will be easy to eradicate. They will stand as an example of our might. Other species will surrender to avoid our wrath. And if we battle them first, we will not face them in every fight as they foolishly come to the aid of the others."

"Who will be next?" Dintral asked.

"When will we know the elves are gone?" asked Ballian. "They may have laid down arms, but they fight to the death when they engage. If we have to kill all of the living elves, we'll need a bigger army."

Vitenkar had thought long and hard about this. Ballian was correct. The elves would not die easily. But they only needed to kill enough to dishearten the rest. "They will only fight as long as they have hope. As soon as they realize there are no more children, they will stop fighting. We will attack the first three villages as soon as the men are in battle condition. By then the elders, at least, will have noticed that there are no more conceptions."

"How have you stopped them?" Ballian asked.

It had been so easy that Vitenkar was tempted to embellish the story. But he decided to save it for the troops. These two men were his trusted lieutenants. They would get the truth. "They are tied to this land. There is a place where their fate is written on a Stone. I have removed this Stone." He didn't tell them that he'd tortured and killed ten seers to get the information he needed to find this place. Or that he hadn't gone himself, but had hired, and then slain, a mercenary.

Chapter 3

Maynard slipped behind the column just inside the meeting room and dropped down to sit in the cramped space behind it. The outer wall against his back, the stones warmed by the sun of late afternoon that beat on the outside, kept him hidden from anyone in the room. He had spent hours here listening to people present contracts, some turned down because the risk was too high, some because the price offered too low. No one was turned down for a contract that skated close to the law if they had the money to pay.

The opportunity to make a copy of the keys had come so out of the blue that Maynard had almost missed it. Now, despite the pain in his muscles from the cramped hiding place, he was glad to have them. Rumors of a big contract had come out of the antechamber this morning. A prominent resident of the island had requested a meeting with the guild board. Having prior knowledge of the negotiations was worth the agony if he could use it to his advantage.

The guild board members entered just as Maynard shifted his body to minimize the discomfort. He couldn't see them, any more than they could see him, but he knew who they were, four of the ten-member board. All of these were human, as was the client. Maynard could replace any of them. And he would when he was more sure of his support. New board members were always elected from the couriers. When Maynard pushed Springheart and Willowvine off the top of the list of couriers, he'd have the support, and then it was just a matter of killing one of the board members. Everyone would vote for Maynard whether they liked him or not.

The small rustling sounds of the four people finding their seats were replaced with some murmuring. The board members were curious. This was a new client and he'd already promised a large fee. If all went well, it meant a substantial increase in the guild revenue. Maynard knew they had plans for opening branch guilds on the mainland and one of the other islands. This contract would go a long way to financing that project.

"No hints of the details?" Elendra, the eldest woman of the group, asked.

Deacon, who was Maynard's preferred target for removal, answered, "There was only a request for a meeting and, of course, a sum of money mentioned."

"Our spies were unable to find any information," Lisseline said. "Aranate Devissial does not often need anyone's assistance. He owns no business that anyone can find. He lives quietly with only two servants. His money comes from his ancestors. I fear we will be at a disadvantage in this negotiation." She sounded frustrated. Her spies were usually able to provide anything she desired in the way of information.

Maynard rubbed his upper lip to avoid sneezing. The rassa tea that dampened his emotions allowed him to avoid getting too excited when he was hiding, but it did nothing for his allergies. He had to find a way to clean this space if he continued to use it. The dust was going to be all over his clothes; now he'd need an excuse for that when he left. While he was distracted, he missed something that the remaining board member said. It was likely not important since it was Reven who had spoken.

A draft of clean air flowed past him. The street door was open. There were two doors, one to the street that the guild board used, and one to the antechamber where clients were screened, and couriers inspected before entering. Clients rarely came directly from the street.

"Citizen Devissial, welcome to our chamber," Lisseline spoke for the guild. "How can we be of service?"

"Please, call me Aranate," the reply came in a soft voice. "I have need of discretion in this matter. I am acting for another party."

"You can rely on our couriers to keep your secrets," Lisseline replied as urbanely as Aranate had spoken. "There has never been a breach of client confidentiality."

"That is why I am here and not hiring my own... couriers."

Maynard winced at the pause. No matter how many times the guild declared their legitimacy, people still thought of them as thieves. Their secrecy only reinforced the reputation that the couriers were on the shady side of the law. That reputation was too close to the truth to ever be fully denied.

"What can you tell us?" Lisseline's voice remained calm, but Maynard knew she felt as he did about their reputation.

"First I have a request. If you cannot fulfill it, I will be forced to go elsewhere, as distasteful as that will be."

No one said anything, but they must have gestured for him to continue.

"My... friend has requested that Springheart and Willowvine complete this contract."

Maynard fumed. It should be the guild board that chose the courier. Clients brought the contract. They didn't determine who would fulfill it.

Lisseline agreed to the condition.

"Very well. The contract is to retrieve an object that has been stolen. It must be returned to its proper place before the next full moon."

"And what is this item?" Lisseline asked. "Do you know who stole it?"

Maynard leaned forward to ensure he wouldn't miss any details. This was critical. If he knew the details before the elves, then he could simply carry out the task and return before they had even started.

"I can only provide the details to Springheart and Willowvine," Aranate said. "Although I feel confident in telling you that part of the contract is to locate the item. My friend knows only that it is on this island, not where, nor do they know who brought it here."

Maynard gritted his teeth. Now he would have to get himself added to the contract. It would have to be done without Aranate knowing. It was too important to Maynard to risk having the contract pulled because he was involved.

"When will you be able to meet with them?" Lisseline asked. "They completed a contract last night. We will need to contact them and ensure they are satisfied with the terms."

Maynard heard a chair scrape against the stone floors. "The payment should be sufficient for you to increase their commission so as to encourage their acceptance. I will return in an hour to meet with them. I will require privacy."

Lisseline agreed and everyone left. Maynard waited until he was sure that the room was empty, rose, dusted his clothes off, and then went to listen at the door. This was the riskiest part of his spying, knowing when and how to leave without being noticed.

There was no sound from the antechamber. It was deserted when the guild met, but would fill with people very soon. Maynard opened the door only enough to slip out.

Chapter 4

Springheart led Willowvine into the guild boardroom. The fact that the board members weren't there was oddly disturbing. The room was far too big for only three people. But it was the only room where they were guaranteed privacy. Aranate Devissial sat in one of the board member's chairs, and he waived them over to join him.

All Springheart knew was that the contract details would have to be kept secret. That even the board wouldn't know what they were doing until the job was done. He wasn't comfortable with the secrecy, but that was the contract, so he'd have to live with it.

Willowvine held Springheart back as he moved to join the client.

"There's a presence," she said.

It wasn't possible. She must be sensing someone outside on the stairs or in the antechamber. "The room has been checked."

She looked at him and he knew she was getting ready to argue. That look was so familiar he didn't need to hear the words. He held up his hand. "It is not possible for someone to be here. The marshal checked the room. Don't argue with me in front of a client. We need to be professional."

Willowvine narrowed her eyes but nodded and followed him to sit beside Devissial.

Springheart knew the argument was just postponed, but he was grateful for the reprieve.

The client was politely pretending that they hadn't spoken. A thin man, his blond hair cut short, his shoulders rounded as if he'd been bent over a book for too long, he radiated calm and civility. Money had a way of making humans more like elves sometimes. Springheart knew that Willowvine would be sensing Devissial's aura. Looking for lies, and dishonest intent. Until the meeting was over, Springheart would act as though the man was dealing plainly with them. When they were done, he would heed her advice.

"You requested us for this job," he said. "Why do you think we are the best?"

Devissial smiled. "Do not pretend that you are not. But it is not your prowess as couriers, or not only that, which brings us together. I am acting as agent for an old friend of my family. He is an elf, and he believes only an elf can complete this task."

Risking a glance at Willowvine, Springheart saw that she was watching the human with no indication that there was trouble. "There are few things that specifically require an elf. When will we get the details?"

Devissial looked down at his hands before responding. "My friend would prefer not to provide details until the contract is agreed. I know that you have the choice and, in your place, I would refuse to commit to something I didn't understand."

Springheart started to respond, but Devissial waved him to silence. "I was told to ask you to take an oath. One that will bind you to secrecy regardless of the outcome of this discussion. Will you both agree to it?"

An oath was something Springheart could agree to, and he knew that Willowvine would do the same. She was practically vibrating with curiosity. Springheart guessed at the nature of the pledge. "The Heart Oath?" Breaking that oath would stop their hearts. It was the strongest oath the elves had.

"Yes."

It was only a matter of a few moments to take the oath, and when they completed the ceremony Devissial settled back in his chair. "How much do you know about the relationship the elves have with Cartref?"

"The health of our world affects the health of the elves," Willowvine answered. "No one has told me anything more. Maybe they tell the non-orphans the details."

Devissial didn't react to the bitterness in her voice. Perhaps he didn't notice, but Springheart felt it and regretted his inability to help her accept their status.

Devissial showed them a sealed message. "I have not been given any other information. But I do have this. I can tell you that something has been stolen that will cause the elves to disappear if it is not returned by the next full moon. I am assured that you have the talent to locate and return this object. If you agree to take the contract, I am to give you this message to open. If you require help during the term of the contract, you may reach out to me." Devissial placed a calling card on the message and then laid them both on the table in front of him.

Springheart wanted to say yes. He knew they would eventually, and that any time spent negotiating was time they wasted. The full moon was only twelve days away and if they had to find the object, as well as deliver it, they didn't have any minutes to waste. He was sure that Willowvine knew what he was thinking because he always took the side of the elves. No matter how badly they were treated by their own people, Springheart would not deny them any request. It was because he knew how hard it was for the elders to acknowledge orphans, let alone ask them for help.

He looked over at Willowvine. She shook her head. Barely a movement, but he knew they would need to talk before they agreed. If he didn't let her speak her piece, they would be arguing the entire contract. They probably would anyway, but it didn't need to be over the elven culture.

Springheart turned back to Devissial. "Before we agree, what are the terms?" Perhaps Willowvine could get some level of recognition. It seemed to him that was all she really wanted, to be acknowledge as someone who has done a service.

Devissial mentioned a sum that would have paid for the whole guild to fulfill the contract. "I assume that the board members don't generally tell the couriers the full payment. I think it important for you to understand the stakes."

"We need to discuss it. Would you allow us an hour?" Springheart hoped it would not take that long, but he didn't want Willowvine to feel rushed. She needed to be fully committed to this. Her oath would protect the secrets, not that they were given any to protect yet.

Devissial agreed to meet them in one hour, took the message, and then followed them out of the chamber. Springheart arranged for a private room in the members' area of the hall.

Chapter 5

As soon as they left the room, Maynard uncurled from his hiding place. He brushed the dust off as he thought about what he'd heard. It wasn't what he'd hoped, but if the two elves needed to take an oath, he was certain that they wouldn't share the contents of the message with him.

He smiled.

It didn't matter. He always had an alternative. He would just convince the board to let him shadow Springheart and Willowvine. They couldn't be happy with the secrecy involved in the contract, and that was something he could use to get the board to do as he wished.

Maynard had forgotten that the girl could sense presences. If Springheart had believed her, they would have found him. He dismissed the thought. It was a worry for later, for now all he had to do was slip out of the room. He placed his ear against the door. He could hear the marshal giving Springheart the number of a private room. Unfortunately, those rooms were too small to provide a hiding place, and they were sound-proof. No matter. It would give him time to talk to one or two of the board members.

Maynard slipped into the antechamber as soon as the voices faded. Luck was with him again and the room was empty. Leaving the antechamber would not raise anyone's suspicions. It was normally a busy room and no one paid attention to who came and went.

He observed the traffic in the public hall. A few clients were waiting to be noticed. Couriers were coming in, going to the private rooms, or sitting in chairs gossiping, or talking to clients.

In a far corner, Lisseline was sitting at a small table taking tea and reading a book. He strode toward her with purpose as though he had an appointment. She looked up as Maynard approached. He acknowledged her greeting and asked permission to speak.

When she nodded, he sat and said, "I understand that we have a new client."

She closed her book and placed it on the table. "Gossip does travel fast. Is there any other information?" Her tone carried suspicion.

Maynard knew she was worried about the news getting out, but since Aranate Devissial had entered through the street door, the fact that he had come wasn't a secret. "No. It seems our eminent client likes his privacy. Have you assigned the contract yet?"

She sipped tea while assessing him. Maynard was used to women looking at him that way. One of his main assets was his looks. He knew that his longish black hair and fair skin drew female attention, and he was usually willing to reciprocate the interest, but today he had more important things to do. He waited Lisseline out, not wanting to appear eager.

After a moment, she placed the delicate cup back in its saucer. "The client has requested a specific courier."

"That is unusual." Maynard restrained his desire to argue. This was his opening. "The board finds that acceptable?"

"We do."

She was keeping everything very close. He had to take care that he didn't give any indication that he knew what was going on.

"May I ask? No, of course that's impudent of me. I'm sure that whoever the contract has gone to is competent — and loyal to the guild."

"All of our couriers are loyal to the guild," Lisseline said. "Why would you imply otherwise?"

"I worry that being chosen by the client will make it more likely that the loyalty will lie with them this time."

Lisseline leaned in to whisper, "Is that how it will work for you, Maynard Slack? Is your loyalty for sale?"

Real anger flushed his cheeks. He pretended that the emotion was offense when he replied, "No. I would never turn my back on the guild. But there are couriers who are less connected to us, ones who have no representatives on the board."

She laughed at him. "You mean Springheart and Willowvine? They will not betray us."

He knew that wasn't true, but a debate on the loyalty of elves wasn't the purpose of this meeting. "I assume that the client chose them. They are the best, after all."

"Do not be so jealous of their status, Maynard. You are one of the best we have as well." Lisseline seemed to consider whether or not she could confirm his guess. "I suppose it will be public knowledge, and I know I can rely on you to be discreet. If we take the contract, it will go to them."

He nodded slowly, trying to give the impression he was considering his words. When he spoke, it was quietly and with an air of concern. "Such an important client, do you not think they deserve more than two people assigned?" He knew the board could afford to have a third person helping, but he couldn't let her know that he knew the value of the contract.

"No. The terms are quite clear. Springheart and Willowvine will be the only ones assigned to the contract. Now, I have a meeting to attend. If you talk to the marshal, you will find a number of contracts that fit your skills."

Maynard rose as Lisseline stood. He wasn't discouraged, just delayed. There would be plenty of time to get added to the contract, plenty of time to find out what they needed to do, and plenty of time to sabotage the two elves and save the day himself.

Chapter 6

Willowvine was determined to make Springheart listen.

As they followed the marshal to the small room at the far end of the row, she imagined the price the elves would have to pay. This contract might be dangerous, so the least they could do was thank her this time.

Maybe she'd ask to be allowed to enter the elven lands again. She could visit her old gang; maybe convince them to form a courier guild that was only filled with elves. People would pay elves to retrieve things, and pay well.

"We are taking the contract, Willowvine," Springheart interrupted her daydreams.

"Of course. I think we just need to ask for more than our usual cut." If she could get him to agree to more money, adding a little retribution for the way they'd been treated would be easier. "The guild is getting enough out of this to double our commission. It would mean some new clothes, maybe a better room."

He shook his head.

She hated it when he did that. She wasn't a child to be

humored. "I'm not saying we should get double, but a bonus would be nice."

"When we joined the guild, we agreed to our commission. It has paid our bills and kept us comfortable. Do you want to risk our position here for a few more coins?"

Taking the fact he didn't outright say no as encouragement, Willowvine continued her argument, "When we joined the guild, we weren't the best couriers they had."

He didn't deny the truth of her statement. He didn't speak at all. Willowvine tried not to get too optimistic. Springheart had done this in the past. He'd let her lay out all her thoughts, and then demolished each one until she was convinced that he was right. This time it was too important for her. She'd been waiting for this opportunity since the day after the battle of the gate.

The elves needed to understand that orphans were not a danger, and the only way she could make that happen was to get them to bring the orphans back in to elven society.

"I think they should give us ten percent as a bonus." She needed to provoke a response. If she could get Springheart to argue with her, there was hope that she could actually win a point.

Money was the easiest thing to talk about. How she would get him to agree to concessions for orphans wasn't clear, but she'd know what to say when the opportunity came.

He waited for her next argument, and Willowvine knew she was losing. "Why not? We deserve something more for this. A bonus would help up set up our own guild."

That got his attention. Springheart frowned and leaned in to whisper, "I have not agreed to do that, and do not speak of it in this hall."

"But if we did, we could hire all the orphans and be just an elf guild." The words just slipped out. It was too late now to dance around the subject, so she continued, "The elves could hire us. You know that there's a need. You did that before we met. If we worked for the elves..." She hadn't thought through the next steps. If they worked for the elves, then maybe there would be less fear of orphans, and that was a step toward being accepted.

"Why do you think the elves would be willing to hire us? It is likely that they would let us set up and then simply arrest the members of your old gang. That they would see it as an opportunity to remove the threat that we represent."

She sighed. That was always the argument she couldn't fight. "What threat do we represent?"

Springheart rose, opened the door, and checked to make sure no one was lurking. Apparently satisfied that they had privacy, he returned to his seat. "I don't know what they think. It's something we represent. There are so few elven children and I have wondered why they would be so willing to ignore us. But then there are not that many orphans. Perhaps a hundred of us."

She stood up and started pacing, trying to burn off the excitement she felt at finally getting an answer. "Exactly! If we were accepted, we could create our own families, and then there are no orphans."

He waved for her to sit. "Have you ever wondered why none of the orphans have had children?"

She started to answer when the import of the question hit her. "No. But there should be, right? We couple and there are enough of us that there should be children." Her earlier argument forgotten, she started to think through the possibilities. "Maybe we need something from our family to make the babies possible. A tea or some other magic, something that we don't get to access."

Springheart shrugged. "We can guess all we want, but we won't know unless someone tells us."

Willowvine sat up.

27

"That's what we could negotiate. The truth about why we don't have children." The other thing could wait. If they could find a way to have children, then the orphans would have a family, and they could rejoin elven society without a plan, or any risk.

"If we knew, do you think it a good idea that we procreate?" Springheart asked.

She knew she hadn't thought through the consequences — again. It didn't matter. If they knew, then they could decide, and think about the results. "Why not?"

"If the elders exile orphans, why would they take in the children of orphans? They would have no family line, they would be orphans no matter that they have parents." He rose with a sigh. "I think we must take the contract as it is. I am not willing to hold the elves hostage to your plans. And the client is not in a position to negotiate anyway."

It was final. And she knew that he was right, but it didn't help. "Fine, we'll do it for the usual commission. But this conversation isn't over."

WILLOWVINE STOOD BACK and let Springheart lead the way as they joined Aranate Devissial in the guild boardroom. This time the board members were in their usual seats, and Devissial sat in the client's chair. Willowvine was irritated that the two couriers were expected to stand as usual.

The presence she felt earlier was still there. She knew it wasn't bleed-over from the antechamber. The aura was muddy so she couldn't tell who it was, but it was too strong to be anywhere but in the room. She didn't say anything because this was not the place to suggest that the guild was not to be trusted. And she wondered if the guild knew and had approved a spy. The board members couldn't be happy with the special treatment this client expected. They were used to being in a position of power in negotiations.

Lisseline took the role of spokesperson. "You have had sufficient time to discuss your options?"

Willowvine almost snorted at the statement. There were no options. Not even the normal one to refuse the contract. The time they'd been given was just a formality. She let Springheart do the talking because he was better at hiding his feelings than she was. Surely he felt the same way, irritated at the politics, annoyed at the pretense, but he was always calm on the outside.

His gaze moved from the board members to Devissial as he spoke, "We have discussed the information we have been given. We are willing to take the contract based on what we currently know."

Lisseline nodded but rather than saying the formal phrases to seal the contract, she turned to Willowvine. "This situation is unusual. We are told that the guild will not know the details. It is important that you both state your acceptance. Do you agree with what has been said?"

It surprised Willowvine to be asked. The guild had always seen them as one unit. Neither of them had ever been offered a solo contract. And Springheart had always been to one to agree to contracts. She had agreed to accept the price, but could she add another condition?

Before Springheart could stop her, she said, "I can't say until we have the details."

Springheart looked at her, barely moving to do so, but her magic saw the change in his aura. The normal calm was turning angry. She had to tread carefully if she didn't want to have a full-blown argument later.

Devissial didn't move, but she saw approval in his aura. Her feelings about what she read were always a part of the deal. A stranger's approval didn't minimize a friend's anger. She shut down the ability, knowing it would only stay quiet for a short while, and concentrated on her goal. "Can we reserve the right to add a condition when we have the details?"

Lisseline deferred to Devissial. "The guild cannot answer for the person you represent."

He considered for a few too many moments for Willowvine's comfort. Even without her power, she could tell that Springheart was getting more angry, and the board members were becoming uncomfortable. Lisseline was regretting the request for both to answer. Willowvine began to think that it wasn't the guild's idea to ask.

"We are both in a difficult situation," Devissial said just as she was about to accept the contract without added conditions. "I do not know what is in the message, so I cannot say what questions you will have. Perhaps we can come to a compromise?"

He waited until she agreed before continuing, "Then let us say that I will speak to my friend. If you have any questions related to the contract, they will be answered. If you have one question unrelated to the contract, I will recommend that it is answered after completion."

She couldn't respond right away. The thought that they would be able to get any information shocked her. She'd been prepared to hear a no, and then accept the contract as it stood.

"I cannot promise more than that," Devissial said when she didn't speak.

Taking in a breath, Willowvine forced herself to control of her excitement. "That is satisfactory. Thank you."

Her power had returned because she wasn't able to control it and the excitement at the same time. Relief was the strongest emotion in the room. Someone was thinking of revenge, but it was lost almost as soon as she noticed it. Her own feeling of victory drowning out any weaker emotion.

Within minutes, the contract was formally accepted, and

the guild members were preparing to leave with their payment. Aranate Devissial approached with the message in one hand and a bag of coins in the other. "I will take my leave. Here are the details, my card, and an advance on your expenses."

Springheart took the items and handed them to Willowvine, annoyance still clear on his face. "We will contact you if we need to. Do you require any progress reporting?"

"You only have twelve days. Do not spend any time reporting. Just get the job done." He turned, nodded to Willowvine, and then left them alone.

Chapter 7

Springheart waited until he was sure that they were alone —
and he had a handle on his anger. She'd promised to accept the
terms. The fact that she'd thought to ask for information, and
that he was happy that they would get at least one answer
didn't mitigate the fact that she'd lied to him.

"I'm sorry," she said before he could express his feelings. "I
didn't expect to be asked. I was caught off guard."

You've had plenty of time to come up with an excuse.

"You aren't that impulsive. You were planning it. We
agreed, Willowvine. That should have been the end of it."

He could see that she was trying to be calm, and to talk
him around, but he didn't need her talent to know how upset
she was because of the tears that made her eyes shine. It was
hard sometimes to remember how young she was. Barely
twenty, which for most elves was still a child.

Willowvine's history and her competence at their job made
him forget that there were still times when she could be hurt.
The elves were her weak point. She badly needed to know that
they valued her, and that she was a person in their eyes.

"I know you think it was on purpose, but, Springheart, I

swear it wasn't. I would never betray you that way." The tears fell and she swiped them away. "I can't be alone, please don't send me away."

He handed her a handkerchief. There was no doubt left, just sorrow. If she believed he'd send her away over this, she was more damaged by the treatment they received than he'd thought. "I'm not breaking up our team. I will never send you away, Willowvine." She wiped the final tears from her eyes and relief, or joy, or something replaced the pain in her eyes.

"That's good to hear. You might have to climb more walls and take more risks if you have to work alone." She laughed. A brittle sound that didn't match the words.

Springheart let her pretense of humor lie. "Can I count on you to not get caught off guard again?" He couldn't maintain his anger in the face of her raw need to be accepted. "It would be a pity to waste your question."

A smile banished the tears. "Yes. We have plenty of time to figure out what to ask. Unless you think we'll be denied. We only have Aranate's word that he will try."

"What did your magic tell you?"

"That he was sincere."

"Then we should prepare our question, but know that we may not get an answer." He looked around the room and then held out the message. "Let's see what exactly we've agreed to."

They broke the seal and laid the message on the table. It was short, and Springheart found himself wishing he'd negotiated a meeting with the real client so that they could get more detail.

Willowvine read the words. "A catastrophe has befallen the elves. You were successful in resolving the last, and so we have commissioned your help for this. The elves are dependent on the Stone of Family to reproduce. This Stone has been removed from its place and if it is not returned, we will die out. Your contract is to locate the Stone and return it to the rightful place. We will provide you with the location where you will deliver it when you have the Stone."

"That doesn't seem like an elf wrote it," she stated. "It's clear and unambiguous. Like they aren't talking to elves at all."

"They are afraid," Springheart said. He knew that without the Stone in place there were only a few centuries left for elves to survive, and as the older generations died without children, more would become the last of their line. When that happened all the remaining elves would become orphans. "I guess step one is to find out who Stole the stone and get it back."

She read the message again. "How will we find that out?"

He had no real answer for that. "We can only hope that the Stone is on this island. Otherwise we don't have a chance. I can only believe that fate wouldn't play such games with us."

Chapter 8

Maynard reflected that his hiding place had been very fruitful yesterday. Now he was the only human who knew the details of the contract. He'd spent a restless night trying to decide which was the better path. To make sure that his rivals failed, which would mean the elves would eventually disappear. It needn't be by natural causes of course. A few assassinations, faked accidents, and an occasional skirmish were all it would take and suddenly humans would be running the world.

The problem with that plan was that he had no reason to believe he'd be one of the humans in charge. The other plan was still the best option. Get involved with the contract, keep his knowledge to himself, and then he could be the one to save the elves. That was a sure way to fame and importance beyond the guild leadership.

For a mad moment, the thought of selling the information crossed his mind, but that was just late night fantasy. It would destroy any hopes he had of becoming a guild board member. No amount of money would make up for that. And he didn't have enough details to satisfy a purchaser anyway. His decision had nothing to do with the twinge of pain in his heart when he considered it. It was simply logical to take the most clear path.

Now that he had made his choice, he had to find a way to get attached to the contract. And it wouldn't be as a partner. The contract and Lisseline were clear on that. Only the two damn elves were allowed to fulfill it.

His appointment with Reven Mistryn was set. After Lisseline he was most likely to have the power to help, and Reven was fond of good food and pretty women. Too fond for his own good. Maynard waited for him in a private room at The Gilded Trout where they would lunch.

"Maynard Slack, my third favorite courier," Reven declared as he strode through the curtain. "A perfect place for lunch. I love the food and appreciate the service."

"The service is especially pretty today," Maynard said, ignoring the resentment at being Reven's third favorite. "I requested Mally. I think she likes you."

Reven sat and moved the place setting slightly to center it. "Then we must ensure my wife never knows about the food, or she will insist that I bring her here to experience it herself."

They exchanged pleasantries while the meal was served, Reven flirting boldly with Mally. Maynard's anxiety had soured his stomach, but he forced himself to eat to avoid suspicion. When Mally left the room for the last time, until dessert at least, Maynard started his campaign. "I find myself at loose ends for the next couple of weeks. I wondered if there was anything I could do to help the guild."

Reven put the rib bone down and wiped his face. "There are plenty of contracts. Someone of your experience should be able to take any of them."

Maynard gave what he knew was a disarming smile. "But the younger couriers need to gain experience. I thought perhaps I could take on a supporting role with one of the larger contracts. Perhaps help out Gayan with the merchant guild contract."

"Gayan already has an assistant. We asked Lorelien to help him. She needs the experience with larger contracts, and he needs watching." Reven didn't elaborate on the reason the board members needed to spy on Gayan.

"I see. Well are there any other large contracts that I can help with? Perhaps train a new courier," he said, careful to avoid offering to help Springheart and Willowvine. That would raise suspicion even in Reven. Maynard would only mention it if the fool didn't make the connection.

"A new contract came in yesterday," Reven said, picking up another rib. "I do not know how large it is, but it seems very important."

Maynard pushed the potatoes around on his plate. "Really. That's odd for a board member to not know the intimate details of any contract."

Reven wiped his mouth and poured more wine for both men. "Part of the deal. I'm sure the gossip has gotten around."

"I know that there was a meeting, and that Aranate Devissial was there. Didn't the contract go to the elves?"

"Yes, by request." Reven stopped shoving food into his mouth and regarded Maynard.

Knowing as much as he did, Maynard had to be cautious of the knowledge he displayed. "I'm sure they are capable. They are a strong team and the top ranked couriers."

"Seemed to be a bit of tension between them," Reven said. He sipped more wine. His second glass to Maynard's half. "It would be good for the guild board to ensure they had all the help they needed."

Maynard nodded at the wisdom. "If they are willing, I can act as their assistant. And I can report any problems to you before the client knows." He added a sly smile to the words.

Mally entered the room with a wink to Reven. She cleared the dishes and then brought small cakes and caf.

"I think that's a splendid idea," Reven said, pushing aside his caf in favor of one more glass of wine. "I will talk to the board and insist that they take you on. But you will report problems to me, not to the whole board. Are we agreed on that?"

Maynard raised his own glass in agreement.

Now let Springheart and Willowvine try to keep him out of the contract. This old fool would be the perfect choice when Maynard was ready for an opening on the board.

Chapter 9

Springheart pushed aside the sheaves of paper that they'd scribbled on during the morning. The guild room was small, but still better than their apartment for this kind of work. It had been a whole day and still they had no idea who had taken the Stone. He hadn't expected much, but one clue would be better than this.

There was still a list of informants to work through, names they'd gleaned from other couriers, people who always seemed to know what was going on. He was starting to think they were asking the wrong questions. It wouldn't work to ask who didn't like elves, too many people were afraid of the unknown. The only common knowledge about his people was that they were berserk fighters. Few outside the elven lands knew about the knowledge, the poetry, or the simple joy in nature that really defined the elves.

Maybe the better question would be who of the local people had changed recently?

A knock on the door of their private room interrupted his thoughts.

Willowvine was interviewing sources, and she was due back in a few minutes, but she wouldn't have knocked. He turned the papers over, and then went to unlock the door.

The marshal waited in the hall. "The guild board wants to see both of you." The man never wasted time on pleasantries with couriers, saving his manners for clients.

"When?" Springheart was not expecting to meet the board. If the client didn't want updates, the board should be hands off.

"Where's the girl?"

"I expect her back soon," Springheart replied. "When does the board wish to meet with us?"

"As soon as she's back come to the antechamber, and I'll put you at the head of the line." He turned and marched away.

This was not a good sign.

After this meeting, they would find a place outside the guildhall to use, so that it would be more difficult to demand meetings, information, or progress.

He locked the door, and started packing the various papers into his satchel. As he finished, the lock turned and Willowvine entered.

"I might have a lead," she said, and then, noticing the tidiness of the room, added, "I thought we had the room as long as we needed it."

"We don't need it any longer," he said, explaining what had happened.

She handed him a sheaf of notes to add to the papers he'd packed. "What do you think they want?"

He shook his head and motioned for her to leave the room. "I hope it is nothing that will require us to give details. The Heart Oath is still in place so we won't, regardless of the consequences. Let me do the talking this time."

The short walk to the antechamber passed in silence. Perhaps she was considering the wisdom of his words.

They were standing in front of the marshal when Willowvine finally responded. "I'll try, but if they want to change the contract, or reduce payment, I won't agree."

"We are not going to renegotiate." Springheart would go to the client if that were the purpose of the meeting. This was too important to let guild politics or greed get in the way. "I suppose I can't ask you to keep quiet if we don't know what's going on. Just don't make things worse."

She grinned, which didn't exactly comfort him, but the door to the boardroom opened and the marshal motioned for them to enter.

Inside the room were only two of the board members. Lisseline and Reven. The red blotches on his face revealed that Reven was his usual half-drunk self at this time of day. They sat when invited, but Springheart couldn't relax until he knew what was happening.

"We have had a discussion," Lisseline said. "The majority of the board members agree that you will need help fulfilling this contract."

The way she said it, Springheart was sure Lisseline wasn't one of the people agreeing to help. Hoping to get her on their side, he asked, "Without knowledge of the details, which we cannot give you, how do you know what help we need?"

"The importance of the client, Springheart," Reven said. "We cannot allow you to be unsupported in this. The client is far too valuable."

Springheart glanced at Willowvine. Her eyes were closed. She was scanning them for intent. Scanning deeply, which drained her energy, and he wanted her to be conscious. He reached over and tapped her arm. She opened her eyes and gave a slight nod. There was no ill intent here, just unwanted help.

"We cannot take on help without divulging details. We have taken an oath."

Lisseline waved away the objection. "This will be assistance. You assign tasks, and Maynard will carry them out. He doesn't need to know any details."

Maynard Slack?

"Isn't he a little too high on the ranks to act as a runner?" Springheart wanted to say no, but he knew that it would just push them to insist.

"He has time, and an interest in helping," Reven said. "I understand there is a tight deadline on this. You need all the help you can get."

They were right about the deadline. He didn't have the luxury of time to sit here arguing a lost cause. They'd find a way to get Slack out from under their feet while they did the work. "When will he be available?" he asked, not quite willing to agree outright.

"Wait, I have a question," Willowvine said before anyone could answer Springheart. "How will he be compensated? I don't think we should pay him out of our commission. We didn't request his help after all."

A good question, but Springheart realized he'd neglected to teach her how to negotiate with more finesse. Dumping all her arguments out on the first round was a sure way to lose the advantage.

"But he will be assisting you. Why should anyone else pay his fee?" Reven was genuinely surprised.

"Because we don't need his help. You are insisting that we take him," she said. "The guild is making a fat commission on this. And Maynard wants to help, you said so."

"She has a point, Reven," Lisseline said. "This was your request. You should bear the cost."

Yes, Springheart thought, Lisseline was opposed to the offer. Perhaps she would be of help if things got awkward with Slack.

"The board should bear the cost. We all voted," Reven argued.

Lisseline glanced at Springheart and Willowvine. "I think this discussion is best held with the other board members and no witnesses. You will find Maynard in the antechamber. Make your arrangements. Do not fail us."

Chapter 10

Willowvine saw Maynard waiting for them in the antechamber as promised, an oily smile on his face as usual.

"Where are we going to meet now?" she asked Springheart in a whisper. "It's not like we can let him see anything we're actually working on."

He took her elbow to slow her pace and said, "Let's find a way to get rid of him for a while. There must be an errand we can send him on."

Willowvine wanted to tell Maynard to go away but knew it wouldn't work. She took the bag containing their papers and waited for Springheart to deal with the problem.

"So, I am at your service," Maynard said as he stepped toward them. "What can I do to earn my keep?"

To anyone it would look like he was only trying to help, but Willowvine knew he was up to something. She couldn't identify the emotion, but a blue stain in his aura tainted the graciousness that he tried to project.

"We need some supplies," Springheart said. "Can you gather them for us?"

Maynard shrugged. "If that is what you need. Do you have a list?"

Willowvine suppressed a smile as a sour yellow blush infused Maynard's muddy aura. He definitely didn't want to be an errand boy. But they needed time to find a way to keep him off their backs, and a long list of shopping would make that happen.

Springheart called her over, and between them they came up with a list of items they needed that would have Maynard running all over town for a few hours.

"Where shall I deliver this?" he asked when they were finished.

Springheart looked around the hall. "We have a private room. I'll have the marshal give you a key."

That arranged, Maynard left them.

"Let's get out of here," Willowvine said. "I don't want anyone listening in."

Springheart led her home. It was only a short walk from the guild, but he was right about leaving the room at the guildhall — home was the best place. They knew the layout and no one could approach them without her seeing the glow of their intent. There were few people around at this time of day and she would expend very little energy keeping a watch out for intruders.

When the door was locked and they were settled around the small table, she felt safe in telling him what she'd felt from Maynard. "He was the presence earlier."

"What?" Springheart was spreading out the notes they had already gathered.

"In the board room, remember? I said that I felt a presence and you said they must be outside?" The emotion she hadn't been able to identify in Maynard was the same that she'd sensed yesterday.

"He must have been hiding in the antechamber. I wouldn't

put it past him to try to spy on the board members." Springheart placed the original message in the center of the table.

"Yeah, like you said, he couldn't have been in the room." She wasn't convinced of that, but there was no point in arguing. "So how do we know what we can tell him?" She didn't want to learn what the oath considered revealing too much by having her heart explode.

Springheart sat and sorted the papers before answering. "I think he knows who the client is, so we should be okay with anything about that. We might be able to ask him to use his contacts to find someone who suddenly has a different attitude about elves." He groaned. "We're much better at retrieving specific items from hard places. Subterfuge isn't our strength, but I fear that it is Maynard's."

Springheart might not be good at sneaking around for information, but this was something Willowvine missed since they'd left the elven lands. When she'd lived with her gang in the hills, they always had to find out where the best items were to liberate. That was her job, along with reading auras, she knew how to find where a treasure might be. "We need to talk to Devissial," she said. "He might have some information he doesn't recognize. And Maynard is good at spying. So, let him spend time asking questions. We can give him a list that includes all kinds of unnecessary information too. He doesn't need to know what we're looking for exactly."

Springheart looked at her and she could see he was impressed. A flash of pride filled her. This was the first time she'd been able to contribute more than Springheart. It made her feel like a partner rather than a student. Maybe now he'd think about her idea of starting their own guild. She laughed and said, "Don't look so shocked. I did this stuff all the time when I lived in the hills."

"I'm sorry that I underestimated your experiences with your gang," Springheart said. "I'll go now and see if we can meet with Devissial today. I don't want to waste time with dithering. We might have to travel with this Stone. You make up the list, and we'll meet in an hour at the guild hall."

She nodded and started creating the questions. Maynard would think he was truly contributing with this. It would keep him busy until late tonight, giving her and Springheart time to do the real work.

THE STACK of supplies that Maynard had left in the guild room was enough to support any expedition. The speed at which he'd delivered worried Willowvine. He might get through the list of questions before they'd thought of another way to keep him occupied.

Now she and Springheart were standing in Aranate Devissial's foyer waiting for their client to join them.

"I need you to read his intent while I ask the questions. Let me know if there's a problem by rubbing your eyebrow.

Springheart was nervous, he'd told her this same information twice on the walk over.

"Don't worry. I think he's telling us everything he knows. If there's anything he missed, it's because he didn't think it was important, not because he's withholding." She glanced around to make sure they were still alone. "Are you going to tell him about Maynard?"

"No."

A few moments later, Springheart greeted Devissial and they retired to a parlor filled with books and small statues. There were small glasses of a local sweet wine and a plate of cookies. Willowvine sat beside Springheart and settled into the light trance she would need to read the client. His aura was all pure honesty.

"We are attempting to locate the Stone, but are having

some difficulty," Springheart said. "If you could tell us more…"

Devissial sipped his wine. "I only have information that will provide you with the final destination for the Stone. I cannot provide you with that until you have obtained it."

Springheart looked at Willowvine but she had no information to add.

"Why us?" he asked.

"I do not know the full reason for my friend's insistence on you. I know that you are very good at what you do, and you are elves. You may be orphans, but you are still preferable to any other being. There is rumor that the Stone is on the island. Oh, I suppose that is new information."

"It helps, thank you," Springheart said. "If it's here, then at least there are fewer places to hide it. What about the size of the Stone?"

"I do not know, but it cannot be too large. It wouldn't be easy to transport. If pressed, I would guess that it's no more than a few feet across, but I don't know."

Willowvine was bored with reading the man's aura. He had no guile, no secret agenda. She kept her attention on the conversation, which continued to be comprised of Springheart asking a question and Devissial answering with an apology but no information. As she looked around the room, the artworks and the number of books Devissial kept captured her interest.

She couldn't see any organization to either collection from her seat, but assumed there must be. The man was a scholar after all. There was a lull in the conversation and she took the opportunity to ask a question that had been bothering her. "How did you come to know your friend? Elves aren't usually that friendly with humans."

"That is true, but we shared a common interest in the history of Cartref. I visited the elven library, and he assisted me with my studies. We became friends and have stayed that way ever since. Well as close friends as a human and elf can be."

It didn't give her any further insight and Springheart wasn't doing any better. It was time to go, but he didn't seem to know that. She turned to him to see that he was still struggling to come up with a question that would help. He really wasn't good at this. Taking pity on him she rose. "Thank you for meeting with us. I think it will all help."

Springheart looked at her sternly, but his aura was all gratitude.

Chapter 11

Maynard followed Springheart and Willowvine through the dim street to the meeting he'd arranged with his informant. It was still early afternoon, but the closeness of the buildings and the height of the walls made it seem like night. It rankled that to meet his goal he actually needed help them this time. But if they never got around to finding this Stone, he couldn't steal it away. And the island was too small for him to get away with simply finding it for himself. Someone, probably a guild board member, would find out and that would mean disaster.

No. His plan had to be getting the elves to do all the work. Then he could finish the job. Not that he could go to Devissial to get the second message, but surely any elf would take the Stone if it was that important — take the Stone and reward him appropriately. Springheart and Willowvine hadn't been properly grateful for his help, but that didn't matter. He'd win in the end.

"Maynard, come walk with us," Springheart called. "You don't need to skulk back there."

He hurried to catch up. He had to keep up the appearance of being with them, even though he was sure they suspected that he had an ulterior motive. "Will you both talk to my informant?"

Willowvine shrugged. "I guess so. We both need to be there."

"I can do the talking if you want," he said. "My informant can get twitchy with strangers."

"I'll do the talking," Springheart said. "But we will all be there."

Willowvine looked at her partner but didn't speak.

"I suppose that makes sense," Maynard said. "You are older, and no matter the species, the young often have difficulty with subtlety."

"Willowvine can be subtle, but she has a different role." Springheart looked at the girl as though she were his best tool.

This was proving harder than Maynard had anticipated.

These two were always bickering, but tonight they had simply agreed when either spoke. If he was going to pit them against each other, he would have to apply more pressure. And they needed to be at odds. It was the only way he knew to make their upcoming failure credible.

He tried another tack. If there was no space for the wedge to come between them, maybe he could force them to worry about him. "You said the details of the contract were secret. Are you sure I won't hear anything I shouldn't?"

Willowvine glanced at him again. It was disconcerting. She seemed to look right into him. That mysterious talent she had, the one that was supposed to be their edge, could it be mind reading?

"Nothing that your informant can say will even get close to the secret," she assured him. "Springheart talks because that's his job tonight. I get to talk plenty, and I'm an expert in subtlety."

Pride. That would be useful. "I'm sure you are." He

paused, trying to give the impression that he was thinking through what she'd said.

"Maynard, we need you to keep up," Springheart said. "Why have you stopped?"

He shook himself out of the pretend fog. "We are almost here. Please don't damage my relationship with Tamm. He is my most valuable asset."

"We know how to deal with informants," Springheart said. "He just needs to answer the question and then we'll be on our way."

Willowvine held the door for them and they entered the dark common room of The Broken Horseshoe tavern. If he didn't need them, it would be easy to have the elves killed in this part of town. And it wouldn't cost much.

When his eyes adjusted, Maynard saw Tamm waiting for them at a table in the far corner. The goblin had a tankard in front of him, and it looked like he'd emptied four or five of them while waiting. It took a lot to make a goblin inebriated, but Tamm was always willing to test the limits. Selling information paid his drinking costs. Maynard hadn't been lying when he said Tamm was his most valuable asset.

Maynard made the introductions and then sat to observe.

"We are Maynard's colleagues," Springheart said. "You have information for us."

"You have my fee?" Tamm always wanted the coin first.

Willowvine was sitting back in her chair, relaxed enough to seem to be dozing. If the child couldn't pay attention for even a few minutes, it would work in his favor later.

Springheart placed the small bag of coins on the table, opened it so Tamm could see the contents, and then pressed his hand on top. "You'll have the bag when we have the information."

Tamm looked at Maynard, injury in his expression. As

much as he wanted to mess with the elves, this was no different from the way Tamm and Maynard did business.

The goblin drank from his tankard before saying, "You're looking for someone who may have changed his behavior lately, correct?"

Springheart nodded.

"Someone who has an unusual level of hatred for your kind."

Springheart waited, and the girl opened her eyes. She nodded at Springheart and then relaxed.

"The name, and any other information you have," Springheart said.

Tamm sighed. "Very well, I suppose I can't expect a nice conversation from elves. The name you want is Byner Lannger. She has suddenly stopped ranting about elves. Not that she was open about it, but those who knew her well were privy to her feelings. Now, she doesn't say anything if the subject comes up."

Springheart looked at Willowvine again. He frowned when she nodded but took his hand off the payment. When Tamm had slipped the money into a pocket, they rose and left the tavern.

Maynard knew he'd missed something between the elves, but he also knew that Byner Lannger couldn't be their target. She wouldn't be patient enough to wait for the elves to die out. If she wanted the elves gone, she'd want it done immediately.

But he couldn't say that. He wasn't supposed to know the details.

OUTSIDE THE SEEDY TAVERN, Willowvine found herself scratching at her legs. The place was riddled with vermin and bugs. She shivered and tried to ignore the creeping feeling on her skin.

"Okay, so we go to this Lannger woman?" She hoped that one of them knew where the woman would be. The whole thing could be over tonight.

"No," Springheart said. "I don't think this is a good lead."

"But he was telling the truth." She'd scanned the goblin and there was no doubt that he was being honest.

Maynard glanced at Springheart before saying, "I think he was, but the woman he mentioned is unlikely to be who you are looking for."

"How do you know?" She tried to scan Maynard again, but his aura was as murky as it usually was. He was always hiding something. She couldn't tell if it had anything to do with the current situation, or whether it was just his normal state.

"Willowvine, Maynard is right. I know this woman and she hates elves, but…"

"But?" she asked before she realized they were treading too close to the details.

"Perhaps I should leave you," Maynard said in his oily voice. "I seem to be making it worse, and there are arguments you cannot make when I am here."

"Good," Willowvine said. She stared at him, waiting for him to act on his offer. She knew she could convince Springheart to check out the lead. Even if she was wrong, it didn't make sense to ignore the only clue they had.

Holding up his hand, Springheart said, "No, stay. We need to think of a better way to gather information." He looked around. "Perhaps not here."

Maynard took Springheart's offer and gave Willowvine a patronizing smile. She saw triumph flash through Maynard's aura.

"You go. I feel like taking a walk," Willowvine said.

"Would your walk take you to Byner Lannger's home?" Springheart asked.

She couldn't lie to him. He had a way of knowing when she did. It was truly annoying. "Not now. Fine. I'll come."

Chapter 12

Springheart couldn't blame Willowvine for arguing. He didn't care for the fact that he was taking Maynard's side. But the lead wasn't good and they didn't have time to follow it. There would be enough good leads to check, if they could find a way to get them.

They left the unsavory part of town to reconvene in The Gilded Trout where Maynard had convinced the owner to free up a private room so they could talk. Creating a new plan would be so much easier if they could tell Maynard more of the details. The man might be sneaky and unpleasant, but he did have a solid network and his skills might be more valuable right now than maintaining the secret.

"I think we are asking the right questions," Maynard said after the waitress delivered their mugs of beer. "Perhaps it is just too optimistic to think the first answer will be the right one."

"There are enough people on the island who dislike elves that we should have more names by now," Springheart said.

Maynard grunted his agreement. "How did you know that

Tamm was telling the truth? If that's not one of the details to be kept secret."

Willowvine looked up from her sulk.

Springheart realized he would have to talk to her later about the value of using people she didn't like. Most of her objection was probably about Maynard taking the same side as he did about the Lannger woman. Springheart could see Willowvine struggling with how much to tell Maynard. It was up to her to explain her power, but he hoped she found a way to keep it secret. There were too many people who would exploit her for it, and some of them were people she considered friends.

"I know when someone is lying," she finally admitted. "I learned how to read their reactions. He wasn't lying."

Maynard narrowed his eyes in speculation of just that exploitation Springheart feared, or possibly in suspicion that she was not telling the truth herself. "He wouldn't jeopardize his standing with me."

"Fine, but I'm telling you he wasn't lying."

Maynard glared at her. Apparently, he had no experience in dealing with other people's obstinacy. "Let me finish. Tamm wouldn't knowingly send us on a false trail. Someone gave him that woman's name to waste our time."

That was a possibility. If the real thief knew they were looking, and it wouldn't be long before that happened with every informant asking questions, then they knew the value of wasting time in this case. Springheart changed the subject from what had happened to what they could do about it. "Can we find out who told Tamm?"

"Perhaps we can be more subtle," Maynard said. He was clearly in his element with this. The veneer of interest he had been wearing since they started was gone, replaced with a real joy. "I hate to use Tamm like this, but we could set a trap."

"Why not just ask him," Willowvine said. "He knows who told him, right?"

Springheart gave her their signal to scan Maynard. He didn't want to be fooled by the man's interest. Maynard still had his own goals. If Willowvine could read his intent, then they would be better armed to avoid a trap. She tapped the table, the code that she agreed. This time she didn't close her eyes, and that meant she'd be weak if it took too long.

"Tamm may get touchy about giving away his source of information," Maynard said. "He worries that I will cut him out. He should be. I thought we could send him on another errand, one that will put him in contact with the same source. We could shadow him." He glanced between the two elves. "You are very good at that."

Springheart watched Willowvine's reaction. Her skin was becoming ashen, but she just shrugged. Perhaps there were people she could not read. He turned back to Maynard. "Can we do that tonight?"

Maynard drank the last of his beer before responding. "No. He'll be too far into the barrel by now. I'll ask the landlord of The Broken Horseshoe to make sure Tamm is sober before the night is over. Now, I need to think a little about the task we should set him. Let's meet here in two hours?"

He didn't wait for agreement, just took his leave through the curtain.

Springheart's dislike of the man returned in full force as soon as he left. He checked the common room to make sure Maynard wasn't listening at the curtain. He saw the swish of a cloak just as the front door closed — Maynard was gone. They had privacy again. Perhaps they couldn't speak plainly, but they could speak more openly now that the man was gone.

"What did you see?" Springheart asked as he returned through the curtain.

"The same as always," she said. "It's all muddy. He's got too many intentions and I can't tell if he's on our side or not."

Her voice faded and Springheart looked more closely in the dim light. She was holding her head on her hand, propping herself up, but losing the battle with fatigue. He called for food and made her eat before they headed for home.

He hoped that Maynard was able to set a good trap, and that whoever was misdirecting them would be the thief.

"THE MESSAGE WAS DELIVERED, SIR," Ballian reported.

Vitenkar swirled the wine in his glass, the ruby liquid clinging like blood to the sides. "And did they fall for it?"

"I was outside the tavern. They knew it was false."

Ballian's attitude would need to be corrected soon. Right now, he was the best option Vitenkar had to keep his plan on track.

Ballian had found that goblin and convinced the sot to pass on the information they had provided. His lieutenant wasn't as useless as Vitenkar had feared. "Did the goblin tell them the full story?"

"I was not inside, but by what they said, it was not the fault of the messenger." Ballian looked over at the liquor cabinet. The hint was not subtle, barely a hint at all. "The girl was fooled, but that was all."

Vitenkar was not going to offer him a drink. This was not a time for celebration. He needed to find another way to send those elves on a foolish chase. If he couldn't misdirect them, the questions they were asking would eventually lead to his door. The Stone needed to be kept away from them for so few days. He couldn't fail at this first step.

"If the girl was fooled, the others can be," he said. "Why didn't they believe?"

That question made Ballian think. Vitenkar wasn't sure if he was thinking about the real answer, or what lie he could get away with. He watched his lieutenant for clues. But when the man finally spoke, it did nothing to assure Vitenkar of his loyalty.

"If I knew where this object is," he said. "I could perhaps create a more intriguing false trail."

There was no need for anyone else to know where the Stone was, or even what it was. He'd gone to the trouble to have it stolen then kill the thief. He would not waste that effort. Until the time limit had passed, no one would be able to betray him.

"If you cannot misdirect a pair of elves and a nosy human, I will start looking for another lieutenant. I'm sure that Dintral will be happy for a second chance to impress me."

Ballian didn't react to the threat.

He had courage. There was no doubt of that. Vitenkar feared that Ballian's loyalty was only to Ballian, and any alliance with another was only temporary. That attitude was not unusual in a Scree lord, but soldiers were sworn to lifelong allegiance to one lord, or were until this damn peace.

After another longing glance at the liquor cabinet, Ballian said, "We need to direct them to someone like you, someone hard to reach, someone who will have a longer-term plan. The woman we used is too impulsive to be credible."

"Who?" Vitenkar knew few people on the island. He'd kept his dealings to business, and usually through agents. He preferred the company of Scree. Even the fools that he'd been able to hire for his army were better than other species. And when he was successful, he could gather a real army, one that could make his plans come to fruition.

"I will do some research," Ballian said. "I will report when I have a name, and a plan."

Vitenkar was angered by the thought that his lieutenant was going to take his leave without waiting to be dismissed. The arrogance displayed toward his superior was a deep insult.

"You may go," he said, to Ballian's retreating form.

Chapter 13

It was night, and Willowvine couldn't sit at the table any longer. There were no new messages, no new plans. If they didn't complete this job, it would be a disaster. She would never have another chance to make the elves understand that orphans were not dangerous, or trash to be discarded.

"I'm going for a walk," she said to Springheart. He told her to be careful and turned back to his list of potential suspects.

Wandering the streets was better than sitting and trying to winkle out a clue from a list of names, but Willowvine was going to make more of the evening than just a refreshing stroll. Tamm may be a good informer, but he wasn't the only one.

The Gilded Trout was a favorite place for informants to gather. They shared information and analyzed deeper meanings to maximize the price. Being so close to the guild, and therefore the informant's most frequent customers, separated the Trout from other taverns and made it much more profitable.

By now almost every informant was aware that she and Springheart needed specific information. If she sat at a table, someone would approach and she would scan anyone who did offer information to know if they were being truthful. Despite what Springheart and Maynard thought, people wanted to help. They wouldn't hide behind a lie knowingly, because it would hurt their reputation. And these informants weren't easily fooled. At least, those who were sober wouldn't fall for a lie.

The common room was almost full. The low murmur of conversation stopped as she walked through the door. Willowvine could feel the eagerness in the room without dropping into a trance. Every man and woman there wanted to be the one to help Aranate Devissial and gain a toehold in his circle of friends. Giving one of the elves a clue would be a fast way of getting his attention. She didn't begrudge them. Reputation was the most important asset in their lives. She would make sure their contribution was recognized.

There was an open table in the far corner. Near the kitchen entrance, it was the least private, and so the last taken. It would work for her purposes. There was enough distance between it and the closest tables that she would have time to scan anyone's intent as they approached.

She shucked her cloak and sat. The excess heat from the kitchen was the other reason no one liked to stay long at this table. The waiter placed a tankard of ale in front of her. "Josie sent it. She said she's got information."

Willowvine looked up and saw Josie crossing the room. One of the few female informants, she was also unique in that she was a sylph. Her magic allowed her to muddle the minds of people who she'd spied on. They wouldn't remember she'd been near.

It didn't work on Willowvine, and her scan of the woman revealed only helpfulness in the sylph's mind.

"I am pleased to see you about the town without your escort. Springheart is formidable," Josie said as she accepted Willowvine's invitation to sit.

"He can be stern," Willowvine agreed. "But you know he values information. Thank you for the intelligence on the ledger."

"It is always a pleasure to be of assistance."

Willowvine nodded, knowing that speeding up the process with the sylph wouldn't help. They had just finished the pleasantries, now she had to wait for Josie to tell her whatever was on her mind. The sylph looked around at the others populating the room, and then back at Willowvine. There was no one lingering, or close enough to overhear, and then sell the information they took.

"You are looking for someone who hates elves, and is suddenly joyful, or perhaps jubilant is the better word. Someone who has changed their behavior recently."

Willowvine nodded.

"I heard two scree talking on this very subject only an hour ago. I have not verified it, but perhaps it will still be of use."

Holding her reaction back, Willowvine nodded again. Knowing that neither Maynard nor Springheart would be interested in rumor, she would have to do the verification herself. "Tell me, and I'll see if it is worth our time."

"I will need payment," Josie said. "I do not ask for the full fee. But it is new information."

Willowvine agreed to a quarter of the fee, almost the entire amount she carried. "Tell me, Josie, and if it turns out to be good information, I will let the other couriers know who helped us."

"Do you know of a man called Ivanston Tollingen? He is a merchant who does business mainly in The City. His home is here, but his business is there. I do not understand how someone can operate a business when their home is a full day away or more depending on the tide and weather."

Stifling her impatience, Willowvine agreed. "Is he on the island now?"

"Indeed. According to the scree I followed, he has suddenly accepted a shipment and is remaining in his house. He is not accepting invitations to any events in the next two weeks."

It was a solid clue. "Do you know where his house is?" Willowvine cursed herself for being so quick to ask. She had no more coins if Josie wanted payment for this.

"Yes, and you will owe me a favor for the answer," Josie said. The smile that accompanied her words told Willowvine that the favor wouldn't be small.

"Fine, I owe you a favor," Willowvine answered. "But only me. Springheart is not part of the price."

"That is fair. Do you have paper?"

Josie wrote an address that was close to the docks. A large home, with a wide lawn, not Willowvine's favorite setting for reconnaissance, but it couldn't be helped. The sylph left after formally ending their discussion with a bow and a wish for their health. Willowvine emptied her beer and took her cloak. As she crossed the common room to exit, the door slammed open and two scree entered.

They were armed and drunk.

One of them looked around the room with the usual sneer they had for any being not scree. His gaze landed on her and the sneer intensified. Then they strode to a private room, shoving the curtain aside and disappearing into the darkness.

IT ONLY TOOK moments to reach the address. This was a small town and it didn't take long to get from one end to the other. Willowvine crouched in the shadow of one of the large shrubs that ringed the property. No wall, but plenty of concealment. The problem was the expanse of grass she would have to cross. And the man had ettran stones placed to light the flowerbeds. Their light spilled in pools across the lawn. It wasn't a completely impossible task, but she knew it would be easier if Springheart was with her.

Holding to one of the sturdier branches for support, she closed her eyes and let her magic seek for anyone within. There were four auras glowing, all inside the house. Two were on the far side; they would not notice her approach. One of the auras was underground, so there must be a basement. Was that where the Stone was being held? The final aura glowed from the back of the building. She couldn't tell what side of the house the person was standing on. Possibly they were in the center, maybe in a bedroom. Unfortunately, her power wasn't able to distinguish whether the person was asleep or alert. She was able to see the wards on the lower windows. The second-floor windows were unwarded, a common mistake that gave her an edge.

All she needed was to get a peek inside. Perhaps the package would be on display. Perhaps there would be an indication of the reason this Tollingen felt the need to stay within the confines of his own residence. The reasonable side of her knew that there were more reasons than a stolen Elven Stone to avoid the public.

She had to take the chance. Going back to let Maynard and Springheart talk her out of it, would only waste time. Sure that none of the people inside were actually looking out, she raced from the shrub to the side of the nearest chimney. Nothing changed, but she could no longer spare the energy to keep scanning auras. She was as blind as any of the other couriers.

Keeping to the shadow of the chimney, Willowvine scaled the wall until she reached an unwarded window. The room inside was dark, and the curtains were drawn. She tugged to test the lock, and the window slid up a few inches. Foolish people. Pushing it open enough for her to slip through,

Willowvine dropped into the room. It was a bedroom, and empty.

There was light under the door in the hallway. It flickered as someone walked past. Leaving the window open, she crept to the door, placing her ear against it. Elves didn't need magic to hear the faintest of sounds.

The footsteps retreated and then descended. The sound of gentle snores came from the right and left. The two auras she'd seen earlier. She inched open the door and waited for someone to react — nothing.

Slipping through, she found herself in a long hall. The light was coming from an ettran fixture; there were three of them along the hall. She slipped back into the room. Now that she was inside the house, she realized the foolishness of not making a plan first.

She would have only a limited time to search for validation that this was the location of the Stone. She wasn't worried about being found out. Avoiding two people wasn't that hard for her. She could hide in places they wouldn't think of, and she was fast. Even so, the longer she searched the higher the risk they'd stumble upon her.

One trip in and out. If she didn't find anything, she'd tell Springheart while Maynard wasn't around — they wouldn't get the chance to gang up on her again.

If she had something to hide, she'd have it as far as possible from any entrance. The basement seemed the likeliest place. Willowvine closed the window, not wanting a breeze to alert anyone that it was open. She'd find another way out if necessary.

Leaning against the door, she verified that there was no one outside. The dash to the head of the stairs was easy, and the stairway had thick newel posts for her to hide behind. Again, no one was in sight.

She scanned quickly, conserving her energy. Both auras were below the ground. Free from worry about getting caught, Willowvine sped down the stairway and searched for a door to the basement. As she tested the first of three doors, voices reached her.

They were coming up from the basement.

She scurried to the kitchen and crawled into the first cupboard she could open. It was as safe a place as any. No one would likely enter until it was time to prepare breakfast. She would have found a way to escape before then.

"Are you certain that it is viable?" A man's voice came to her.

They were coming to the kitchen.

Footsteps passed and a door opened. She heard the flick of a flint, and the aroma of flavored herbs drifted toward the cupboard. She was going to be here until they finished their pipes.

"Yes, and it will hatch within a few days. You'll imprint on it over the next week." The second voice was female.

Whatever they were hiding, it wasn't the Stone. Willowvine kept listening. There were few creatures that would imprint on a human. Knowing what they had might come in handy.

"I do hate this forced imprisonment," the man said. He must be Tollingen. "I know it is my home, but I get bored. And with only the servants around, I have no outlet. Would you consider staying, my dear?"

"I must not be here, Ivanston. I have had too much contact with the egg. This is my last visit until you have imprinted the creature. If I stay, there is a danger that the gilhawk will imprint on me. You would not want that." The woman's words carried a tone that said she wouldn't want a gilhawk.

Willowvine didn't blame her. The birds were hard to handle even when they imprinted. Tollingen would have to be careful of his pet. He'd be responsible for any damage it did.

Now she just had to wait out their pipe smoking and get back to Springheart. At least they could cross one name off the list.

Chapter 14

Springheart looked out the window. The night had deepened while he'd been poring over the many details that various informants had provided. Unfortunately, all the details did was muddy the picture rather than illuminate the answer.

There was no one on the street. That was a worry. Willowvine should have been back by now.

He knew that she'd been upset. He hadn't enjoyed agreeing with Maynard Slack, but she was too inexperienced to know when something wasn't right. That was his fault. They had fallen into a pattern of him leading and her following. He should be teaching not leading. He would have to change, or she'd end up in some kind of trouble that he couldn't fix.

Springheart returned to the table and stacked everything in a pile. There was nothing more to be learned from the notes. Perhaps Maynard would be able to come up with something. And hopefully they would find a way to disengage him from the assignment soon, before he learned too much.

Springheart took his cloak and sword from their place on the wall. Everything in the room was within reaching distance.

It was convenient, but perhaps they should find larger accommodations. Living on top of each other had been bad enough before, but now they argued so often that a little privacy would be good.

Springheart told himself he wasn't worried, that the twinge in his gut was just hunger. He left the rooming house and turned toward The Gilded Trout. There would be someone there who might have information, and the food was acceptable. He could bring back a meal for Willowvine when he was done.

The common room of the Trout was half empty. He nodded to a few people he knew, but didn't encourage anyone to join him. He would eat and then go looking for Willowvine. If someone had something to say, they could join him. He had no time for the gossip that usually filled the tavern.

Before he reached an empty table, he felt a touch on his arm. Struggling not to react with his sword, he turned slowly to see Josie standing behind him. "Springheart, good evening to you."

He didn't want to engage in sylph small talk, but he couldn't be rude. "More night than evening, but I hope yours is interesting and profitable."

A smile grew on her face, the expression conspiratorial. "It has been so far. Was my information useful?"

Springheart motioned to an empty table. If Maynard had information and hadn't passed it on, then he would be easy to remove. "What information?"

A green tinge touched Josie's cheeks. "I am not sure I should say. Willowvine paid me for the information and her favor is on the line."

Willowvine?

If she had information that he didn't, it could only mean that she was following up on it. That was dangerous. Whether the information sent her to the Stone or not, they were investigating people who hated elves. People who would love the opportunity to hurt her or kill her for entering their homes. "We are working together, Josie. I must have missed her at home. Can you tell me where I might find Willowvine?"

The green blush faded as a smile of avarice stretched her mouth. "I can, but I will require payment. It would not be good for my profits to be known as someone who gave information for free."

"What is the price?" Courtesy pushed aside in his haste to find Willowvine, Springheart waited.

The sylph assessed him. "I think it would be to my advantage to have a favor owed me by the two best elven couriers. I have one from Willowvine, would you owe me one?"

He nodded and gave her the required response. "Now, where can I find her?"

"Ivanston Tollingen's house. Do you know it?"

He did. The man's name had been on their list. "Why would she go there?" He asked it of himself, only realizing he'd spoken out loud when Josie responded.

"Willowvine paid cash for that information. On second thought I think it best to tell you. He is hiding something in his home. And he is not leaving for at least two weeks."

Springheart gave Josie a few coins as a thank you for the information. The money that Devissial had provided was far more than he'd expected, a little generosity would likely reap benefits later.

He crossed the town in a few minutes and stood in the shadow of a doorway across the wide boulevard from the house. It looked like a fortress. The only lights visible were the ettran stones placed in the flowerbeds. If Willowvine had gone inside, he would have to follow, but this was her strength not his.

Perhaps she was watching the house from the hedge. He

didn't hold out much hope. Willowvine was not that patient. He ran across the road to melt into the shadows under the shrubbery.

This side was the best for surveillance, the boulevard lay empty and the moonlight shone on the other side. If she were watching the house, she would be near. If she'd entered the house, she would have started from here.

A rapid search of the area revealed no Willowvine, but he found the place she'd waited. Her footprints were plain to him, but would not be to a casual observer.

She was in the house.

Springheart pushed all thoughts of what might be happening to her aside. Crouching in her footprints, he tried to figure out her path. He didn't try to figure out her plan, because he was sure she didn't have one. Another thing he should have taught her rather than just done for her.

Looking across at the building, he decided that she must have run for the shadow of the chimney. If she got inside, that meant there were unwarded windows. He didn't have the magic to see the wards. That was her role. He would just have to run to the chimney and hope for some clue. As he prepared to make the crossing, he noticed movement. Someone was climbing down from a second-floor window — Willowvine.

And someone else was strolling around the building.

If she didn't notice, then she would be caught. He knew she couldn't climb and scan for auras, so she might not know. The grass would muffle the person's footsteps so there was nothing to alert her.

He whistled their warning code. A gull, which should go unnoticed by anyone else. She froze on the wall. Unless the person walking the grounds looked up, she would be safe. If he did, she could move faster than a human. It would be a chase, but she would win.

Springheart held his breath as Willowvine inched along the

wall, taking the chance that no one would be looking up, to move into the shadow of the chimney. He feared that she would slip, that something would fall and catch the attention of the human. Willowvine saw the human right then and froze again.

The figure stopped. Springheart slid his sword from the sheath. If he had to, he would attack.

Holding something to his mouth, the human flicked a flame into being, lighting a pipe, and effectively ruining his night vision. Willowvine would be safe unless she fell into the man's arms. When the pipe was burning steadily, the human walked on. As soon as he turned the corner, Willowvine descended and ran across the lawn.

"Are you insane?" Springheart whispered.

"No, but I eliminated Tollingen from our list."

Springheart glanced around to make sure the street was clear. "Tell me later. We need to meet Maynard. Perhaps he can do something more than just take incredible risks to eliminate someone."

She ran when he indicated it was clear. From behind he noticed the tense muscles of her back. He didn't need magic to see the anger blazing from her like a beacon. She'd frightened him, and he'd reacted badly. It was going to take more than a simple apology to set things right.

When they were safe on the street leading to The Gilded Trout, he held her elbow. Her muscles were like rocks. "Wait. We can't meet Maynard this way. I am sorry. You did take a risk, but it was worth it and nothing bad happened."

She glared at him, but the anger was already leaving her muscles. "I knew what I was doing," she hissed back to him.

"I know." He let her arm go. "I know you can do these things, but please don't surprise me like that again. I may not survive." He saw her take in his humor as the anger left her glare, to be replaced by a rueful smile.

"Well, I have to admit, it would have been good to have you there. I had to hide in a kitchen cupboard. It was full of moldy flour. I'll be smelling it for weeks."

Chapter 15

The elves were late. If this is how they run their jobs, he wouldn't need to try too hard to knock them off the top of the list.

Maynard had arranged a private room this time. Sitting in the common area gave him itches. There were too many people in there. If someone wanted to speak to him, they could ask for permission to enter the room. Mally would send the elves in as soon as they arrived. He had little more to add to their knowledge, and he was tired of this slow gathering of useless information.

He was going to make another suggestion for finding out what they needed. The elves were good at breaking into houses. They could do so with all the names on the list within a few days. That was the only way they were going to find this Stone. The only way he could take it and the glory of fulfilling the contract.

The curtains moved aside and Willowvine entered followed by her partner. Maynard smiled at them, making sure that his annoyance was hidden. He still needed to keep them sweet. "Ah, I hope you have had better luck than I tonight."

Springheart held out a chair for the girl. She looked even more pale than usual. Elves always looked a half-day dead to him. That translucent skin rarely showed color.

"I've ordered food," Springheart said. "We'll talk when the meal is on the table."

Mally delivered the order within a few minutes of their arrival. As soon as she left, Maynard said, "Tell me what you've learned. I know something has changed. Please, don't keep me in suspense."

They looked at each other, and he knew there was a secret they wouldn't share with him. If it got in the way of the contract, he'd find out what it was no matter what the elves wanted.

"You tell him," Springheart said to the girl.

She was stuffing her face and held up a finger to get them to wait while she chewed and swallowed. Her manners were unbelievable, but at least now she was looking less dead. Maynard filled her glass and waited until she was ready.

"I've eliminated Tollingen from the list."

Surely, she could give more details than that after making him wait. "How?"

Springheart touched her arm when she seemed about to snap at him. "There are things we can't tell you, Maynard. You know that. Accept that the man is not who we need and tell us what you have learned."

The elf was arrogant, like they all were. "Of course, I was simply curious. If you believe that he is eliminated, then that is what he is."

Maynard knew that he couldn't just baldly state his recommendation, but their news opened a door for his plan. "I was unable to get any further information. Tamm is currently unavailable. I was too late to stop him from drinking himself unconscious. We will have to wait until tomorrow to ask him anything. The landlord of the Horseshoe will alert me."

Maynard took a sip of his wine. The vintages were excellent here, and the client's advance needed to be spent on something pleasurable occasionally. "I have an idea," he said after savoring the fruity notes of his drink. "It may take us some time, but if we act separately, then we should make progress. I'm sure you'll agree that it's more than we're doing now."

"I'm interested in any idea," Springheart said.

The girl looked at him and shrugged, continuing to shovel food in her mouth.

"This list we have, the target is on there, correct?"

Again, the look between them. Willowvine answered this time. "We believe so, but there is always the chance that we are missing someone."

"Let us assume for now that the list is complete. If we split the list and reconnoitered each location, homes, and warehouses, etcetera, we can eliminate names until we find the one we need." He waited for their response, anticipating their arguments and aligning his own.

"It is a good plan, but we cannot split up," Springheart said. "I know you think you can persuade us, Maynard, but there is no way. We cannot give you enough details to allow you to effectively eliminate a name. And, after tonight, Willowvine and I are not going to work separately."

So, something had happened and the girl worked tonight on her own. Not surprising that she caused a problem. She was impetuous. "Then can you tell me what to look for without giving details? I know you are the best at slipping in and out of houses, but I know how to do it as well."

He was getting tired of them giving sidelong glances before they spoke. He knew the risks. Even if they didn't know that he knew, he still needed them, at least until they found the Stone. He waited until they decided what to tell him.

Springheart spoke this time. "We cannot tell you any more

than we already have. We'll start the reconnaissance tonight, but we can only do it ourselves."

There was no use pressing. Maynard would do as he pleased anyway. "Then what can I do? I want to help. This is important enough to the guild that they assigned their top three couriers to the contract."

"You were not assigned to the contract. You were assigned to us. Now, let me think," Springheart said. "We are not trying to be obstructive, but there are terrible consequences to sharing the wrong details."

This was the wrong way to get what he wanted but Maynard's patience was gone. Before he said something that he would regret, Maynard needed to get away from this pair. "Perhaps you need time to discuss it," he said, rising. "I will be back in a few moments."

Springheart thanked him and turned his attention to making sure Willowvine was feeling well, leaving Maynard no option but to go through the curtain.

SPRINGHEART CHECKED to make sure no one, including Maynard, was lurking at the door. The oath wouldn't care if they disclosed details accidentally. It would still kill them.

"I hate to admit it, but Maynard has a good plan," he said. "It worked already."

Willowvine stopped eating and grinned. "Yeah a great plan. There are twenty people on the list, remember. That's at least twenty break-ins. Some of them will have more than one place they might store the thing. And there's no guarantee that the thief would keep it at home."

"Maybe we can send Maynard in as a spy. He could try to ingratiate himself with the people who hate us."

She laughed. "Who is to say he isn't already part of that group. You've seen how he looks at us — me especially." She stacked the empty plates and put them on the sideboard. "We need to send him on an errand to get him out of our way. If we work at it, we can cover the homes in a night."

"It would be too risky to move that fast. We need to think this through. Find an order for the names that makes it more likely we'll be successful quickly."

Willowvine shrugged. "Okay so we take a few nights to search buildings. The full moon is far enough away that we can take some time. If there was a long journey to replace the...it then Aranate would have known."

Her logic was sound. Springheart hated this secrecy. The elves would be better served in the short run if more people could be told. He knew that would place the Stone in jeopardy when it was replaced, but surely it could be guarded. And if the location was so secret, how could it have been stolen?

"What can we get him to do?" he asked. Maynard was slippery and they needed a solid plan.

"Why not get him looking where the people on the list have been in the last week," she said. "It might help eliminate some of them without breaking in. We don't need to give him any more information than he already has."

At least she had skills when it came to the art of distraction. He opened the curtain and called the waitress to take the plates and bring more wine. It might help Maynard to believe in the assignment if he had a little more alcohol in his system. He and Willowvine would stick to tea. They could fit one more name on the list in tonight if they hurried.

Maynard joined them as Mally left the room. Springheart drew the curtain and explained the plan.

"You think that knowing where these people were in the last week will help?" Maynard asked. "So, they have brought something to the island?"

"Maynard, stop trying to get information from us. Believe me, we've told you everything we can, and if we learn more that we can share, then you will be told that too." Springheart was tired of the guessing game. The man didn't know about the oath, but he should accept that they couldn't tell him anything and get on with the job.

"I apologize," Maynard said, not looking at them. "It is difficult to help when I know that I don't have all the information."

"Will you do it?" Willowvine asked.

He swirled the wine in his glass and then looked at them. "Of course. I know how important this is. I'll find out where these people were every moment of the last two weeks. Will that be sufficient?"

To Springheart the words seemed to drip insincerity. "Good, then we have a plan. Shall we meet tomorrow morning to compare results? Eleven? Here?"

Maynard looked at Springheart for a long time and then turned to Willowvine. Springheart knew the man was suspicious, but without any special power he could only guess that they weren't being completely honest. Finally Maynard nodded. "It sounds like a good plan."

Willowvine stood and slid the fresh bottle toward Maynard. "Enjoy the wine. We have business elsewhere."

Springheart followed her out, trying unsuccessfully to stifle the smile at her imperious attitude. Maybe she had it right. Not giving Maynard Slack an opportunity to argue saved time.

Chapter 16

Willowvine looked at the scrap of paper that held the names of their suspects. Two more crossed off last night, but they still didn't know who took the Stone.

The laxity of the security in the homes and business properties still amused her after all the times she'd broken into and out of buildings. There was rarely a guard, and when there was, he tended toward ancient. It helped their work, and she guessed the business bottom line, but if there were any thieves around, the inventory would be gone. The only house warded had been Tollingen's and that might have been new to deal with his pet.

Now, she and Springheart had split up despite his reluctance. He was talking to the harbor master's assistant, and she was supposed to be checking the rest of the buildings to make sure they could be efficient in their search. Knowing the best entrance and exit points would save them enough time to get four, maybe five, names off the list tonight.

The idea to talk to the assistant had been hers, and she hoped it would show Springheart that she did know how to think ahead. If Maynard was checking travel times, it made sense that they should check on possible escape plans. Anyone with a ship would be able to slip away with little notice. The Stone might have come from off-island, in fact probably had. This island was populated enough that there were few places to hide an artifact with such significance. It wouldn't be sitting on the side of a road, part of a dry fence. The elves would have made sure there was a whole ceremonial site. There was probably a stone spiral path, like the gate between worlds.

She still had an hour before they were scheduled to meet Maynard, and two more locations to scout. The houses were all done, but they had plenty of other places to reconnoiter. The final buildings were a warehouse and an office building on Wharf Street. Both only had side and front entrances, the backs made of solid stone wall, no windows, no delivery doors, nothing. She wondered how merchandise was delivered, but perhaps the items were small enough to go through the obvious entrances. Regardless, they would have to come as late as possible when they searched to avoid being seen entering.

Willowvine sat at a small table outside a cafe, facing the corner of the office building. She sipped the mug of caf she'd ordered and made a sketch of the building. In case anyone was checking on her, she had a number of sketches in the same book, allowing her to masquerade as an art student.

This building would be easy. The challenge would be getting through the search quickly. It was three floors and all of it belonged to the same business. She turned the page and started a sketch of what she could see of the warehouse next to it.

The waiter approached her table. "Is there anything more?"

She flipped the book face down and ordered a refill of her caf. That should let her stay at the table long enough to finish her sketch.

While she waited, people started to fill the tables wanting a mid-morning break from business, or whatever else they did so early in the day.

Two scree took a table across the patio from hers. Their conversation in progress drifted to her.

"Yes, but he pays on time, so if I have to take the bloody training again, I will."

"We already know more about battle than he does," the second scree stated in the tone of an old argument constantly rehashed, never settled.

"His lack of knowledge means he pays better than most. He doesn't know the going rate. And it's only for a handful more days, then —"

The waiter moved between Willowvine and the scree asking another table of patrons for their order. His words blocked the conversation just as it was getting interesting. Frustrated, she strained to hear, but couldn't make out anything.

When the waiter moved away, she heard, "…and then we can get on with the next stage."

The second scree huffed, but his words were lost to her as the waiter refilled her mug. She bit back the request to leave her in peace and dropped coins on the table to pay the bill so that she could simply walk away if needed.

"Ballian never talks about those meetings you have. Are you brewing some great battle up there?" Was the next statement she heard.

"Well, I can't really talk about it either. Vitenkar trusts us, not that he shares the details of the campaign. He wouldn't want me to blabber his business all over the place if he did."

Vitenkar was on their list. She'd scoped out his home this morning. He kept everything close. The first floor of his home held a warehouse, servants, and what looked like a barracks. The second floor was where he lived. They were going to have difficulty getting in and out quickly with that one.

"So, you aren't going to tell me what this ..." his words were drowned out by a baby's wail.

"No, and don't name it out here in public, or he'll confine us to barracks."

Willowvine wanted to lean closer, to move to a nearer table, anything to get the full conversation. This was the first real clue she'd gotten. Springheart would want more proof before he did anything about it, but it fit.

She watched as the two scree downed the hot dark brew of caf. When they finished, they rose and left the patio. She slipped the sketchbook into her bag and trailed them, too far back to hear their conversation, but afraid to get closer because they might notice her.

They were headed back to Vitenkar's house. Willowvine considered a shortcut. A hand touching her shoulder stopped her from taking the turn. She whipped around ready to defend herself to see Maynard Slack standing there, the oily smile aimed at her. How long had he been behind her? Had he heard them talking at the cafe?

"Willowvine, are you going back to the tavern? May I walk with you? We'll be a little early, but it will give us a chance to talk, get to know each other?"

She wanted to tell him to go away, but the scree were gone. She'd learn no more from them. "Fine, let's go. Maybe Spring-heart will be there already."

Maynard wouldn't get any information out of her no matter what he wanted to talk about.

Chapter 17

Springheart entered the private room they'd booked to find Maynard and Willowvine already there. The two were sitting facing each other across the table, actively not talking. Willowvine had her elbows on the table, chin resting on her palms, glaring at Maynard. He sat looking at the ceiling ignoring Willowvine.

"What do you have to report," Springheart asked. It would be better if they just got it over with. He didn't have the energy to mediate whatever they were fighting about.

Maynard turned his gaze from the ceiling and tossed a stack of papers on the table. "Here is what I found. They all traveled to The City. Four of them were off island for more than a week. Does that help?"

Springheart knew that Maynard was still digging for details even without asking specific questions. "I'll read through it, thank you." He turned to Willowvine. "Did you scout all the buildings?"

She gave another glare at Maynard and then placed her sketchbook on top of the pile.

Springheart would have to find out what they'd argued

about, but it could wait until later. "Anything we need to know about without reading through the whole pile?" The stack of information was more than he'd expected.

She flicked at glance at Maynard. "I'm not sure I can tell you what I learned."

The man rolled his eyes. "Will five minutes suffice?"

When Springheart nodded, Maynard left. Willowvine checked to make sure he wasn't lurking this time. This contract was only made harder by Maynard's presence. They met in the inn because Maynard couldn't be trusted not to search their rooms if they met there, and a room at the guildhall was private, but not secure, too many nosy and ambitious couriers around. Springheart itched to make progress and he feared that this interference would make him do something stupid just to move forward.

"Well, what did you learn?" He knew that Maynard would be back at the last second of the time he'd given them. He seemed willing to get the contract done. Perhaps he was as frustrated at the need for secrecy as Springheart.

"I overheard something and I don't know if it gets too close to the details," she said.

And you don't like the man. "Well, we are alone." He would trust her feelings until she proved that she was just being petty as he suspected.

Willowvine relayed the information ending with, "I don't know if he heard anything, but Maynard found me while I was following. So, this Vitenkar must be the one, right?"

Her information was good. Vitenkar was now the number one suspect. That meant they needed to get rid of Maynard for the night. If he tried to come along it would mean their death when they found the Stone. Regardless of his desire to rush forward, Springheart knew that Willowvine needed to learn how to work with people, even people like Maynard Slack.

"And why were you both acting like sullen children when I arrived?"

"He wanted me to tell him what I found. And when I wouldn't, he started sulking."

Springheart was sure that there was more to the story, otherwise she would not have been sulking too. "And?"

"And maybe you should ask your new best friend." Arms crossed over her chest, Willowvine shut the topic down.

There was a knock on the doorframe and then Maynard joined them again. "Is it safe for me to enter?"

Springheart waved him in. This was difficult. Now they had to find a real task for Maynard, one that would keep him away from them tonight. One that wouldn't seem like he was being fobbed off. The last resort was to go to the guild board and say they had reached a point where all the information was confidential. It wouldn't guarantee that Maynard would be pulled off the contract. It might mean he'd be there covertly. If they had to keep looking for spies, then the contract would fail, they would die, and so would the rest of the elves. Even if that death was years, even decades in the future, knowing that it was the end of the elves would mean life simply became time spent waiting to die.

"We have all the information we need, I think." He watched Maynard for signs of argument. The man was nodding, his expression open and agreeable. Springheart couldn't suppress a suspicion that Maynard was just pretending. "The bulk of the work now needs to be done at night. So, here's what I propose. We each take a list of homes, and spend the night observing the comings and goings. By morning we should have reduced the list to a more manageable size."

"We have wasted two days, and now you are willing to waste another?" Maynard asked. "I thought there was a hard deadline."

"We have not wasted any time. What would you have us

do? Charge into fifteen homes of the most prominent merchants on the island?"

"Of course not," Maynard shrugged, a lazy and insolent response. "This sniffing around is not what I expected. I thought you were both experts at entering buildings. I thought we would be searching."

"You are thinking a lot for someone who doesn't know all the details," Willowvine snapped.

Holding up a hand to quiet the argument that was about to burst out, Springheart said, "Barging into people's homes doesn't require preparation. Slipping in and out unnoticed requires a great deal of it. Does anyone have any suggestions?"

Willowvine looked about to offer something. Springheart glared at her and she slumped back in the chair. Maynard waved for Springheart to continue.

"If we share the list, we will have to enter four houses each and two or three other buildings. We should be able to accomplish that tonight. Maynard, you will just gather intelligence and report back. You are looking for any secretive behavior outside normal business practices."

"Very well, and if either of you find what you are looking for, what will you do?"

Springheart knew what they would do, but he couldn't tell Maynard, first because it would reveal too much about the Stone, and second, because the elves were not splitting up. "The same, but since we have the details, we will know when we are successful."

"Give me my information and the sketches she made. We should rest for the remainder of the daylight and I think meet again at dusk."

Maynard's attitude annoyed Springheart and made him more sympathetic to Willowvine's ill temper. Not buying into an ego battle for control, Springheart culled the information from the pile and waited until Maynard was gone before arranging the rest of the papers to put Vitenkar's information on the top of the pile.

THE ELVES WERE naive if they thought he would slip off and leave them to work alone. The girl had been following those scree. Maynard didn't know why, but he knew who the fighters belonged to. The research he'd done revealed that Vitenkar had been hiring mercenaries for the last two weeks. He hadn't thought much of it, scree tended to like warriors around. Most families had a standing army, but there were always fighters who preferred to sell their loyalty. Scree mercenaries ran the gamut from those who had failed to act fierce enough to those who wanted more battles than the occasional family skirmishes.

Now that Willowvine had shown interest, the information he'd gathered seemed more pertinent to their quest.

The scree had the Stone. He was sure of it. There was no single piece of information pointing to Vitenkar, but it fit.

Maynard also knew the elves would be searching the premises and not splitting up to investigate other locations. There had to be a way for him to help, or appear to help.

Let the elves obtain the Stone, take all the risks, and then he'd take it from them and get the glory of saving the elves and fulfilling the contract. Maynard couldn't be there tonight, but he could perhaps lower the odds of them getting caught.

The scree would be in the gambling houses. In peace, as short as that usually was in scree society, they channeled their adrenaline addiction into gaming, usually dice and cards.

There was a gaming house not far from Vitenkar's residence. Maynard formed a plan as he walked. He could draw the majority of the mercenaries away tonight without the elves knowing he was involved.

Vitenkar wouldn't know that Maynard had abetted the

break-in, which meant the scree merchant could be used later if things went wrong. Or, a better idea, when the elves had the Stone, perhaps he could trick the scree into helping him in his plan to take it from them.

Maynard liked to use all of the opportunities that came his way.

Chapter 18

Willowvine followed Springheart from the tavern. She wouldn't be able to rest and didn't need sleep to be successful tonight. They were going to walk the perimeter, or as much of it as possible, of Vitenkar's residence. This would not be as easy as last night's searches.

Scree weren't lazy, and they guarded what they valued.

She wanted to talk to Springheart, to discuss their approach, but he was lost in his own thoughts. She scanned ahead and saw Maynard turn down an alley ahead of them. Willowvine touched Springheart's shoulder to get his attention and told him what she'd seen. "His home is the other way. He isn't going to do as he agreed."

Springheart stopped and observed the entrance to the alley "Can you scan him?"

Willowvine closed her eyes and sought Maynard's aura. There were a lot of people around creating pools of auras in buildings. A bright blotch of anger ahead at their destination didn't worry her. Scree were always angry. She'd be concerned when that changed.

There was another blotch of anger shaded with excitement

at the end of the alley. All she could see of Maynard's aura was the usual muddiness, but he was joining with the other auras. Sighing as she returned to the physical world, Willowvine said, "Nothing new. What's down that alley? There is a bunch of scree there."

Springheart started walking toward their destination. "Gaming houses. Perhaps Maynard Slack is the type of man who relaxes with dice."

It was frustrating to deal with the reality that her power wasn't going to help. It was her advantage, but it didn't work. She knew that trusting Maynard was a mistake, but without any evidence, even weak evidence, Springheart wouldn't jeopardize the contract. "I bet he's going to meet some scree. I think he's up to something. He knew I was following them. We should check on him."

"It's more important for us to be prepared tonight," Springheart said. "We're both going in, and we need to know how much danger we might face. Maynard's vices have nothing to do with us."

"It would only take a minute to see what he's doing. If it's just gambling, we can continue." Why did he always think she was wrong?

Springheart came to a stop and looked back to the entrance to the alley. "Can you tell how many scree are there?"

Where was he going with this? "No. Just that there are a lot."

"Can you tell how many scree are at Vitenkar's from here? It's only a few streets away."

She closed her eyes and checked. "A lot," she answered after a second look at the auras.

"More than in the gambling house?"

"Yes. What exactly does that have to do with it?"

"They will probably all be at home tonight. No scree would allow his army to waste time on games and drink. They would be in constant training. That's why I want to see what we're up against. The scree in the gambling house aren't going away. Maynard Slack isn't trying to make us fail. It would ruin his reputation as well. The house is only a few minutes away."

"Fine," she said and started walking toward Vitenkar's house.

Springheart stopped her. "We'll check the house and then go back to see what Maynard is up to. I don't doubt your ability, Willowvine. I just think we need to deal with the contract. Maynard has his own agenda, I know that. But he doesn't have any of the information he would need to betray us."

She couldn't muster any valid argument. She hoped they weren't making a mistake. Maynard Slack was not to be trusted. "Fine. Let's do this fast."

Vitenkar's home was enclosed behind a wall. It was too high for them to see over, and far enough away from the neighboring buildings to make it obvious if they simply strolled around. Willowvine scanned the building again, but there were too many people there. She was able to distinguish that the women were in the back of the house, probably servants. There was a mass of auras on the left of the building, and a couple of them upstairs on the same side.

"Probably business downstairs, personal upstairs," she said. "What if we go to the hill and see if there's a way through the back, maybe the kitchens?"

The hill she pointed to was close enough to the back of the house to let them see in, far enough away that no one could use it as an advantage in a fight. The scree were always prepared to defend from attack, even in a town as peaceful as this.

"It is going to be a challenge tonight," Springheart said. "We'll be going in blind. I don't like it."

They strolled to the hill and rested below a large oak. "I'll climb up and look. We'll only see the back, but there are fewer scree there," she said.

Not waiting for him to argue, Willowvine scaled the ancient tree. The branches were sturdy enough to bear her weight even at the tapering ends. Peering through the leaves, she memorized the few details she could see.

Dropping straight from the branch to land on the ground, she said, "We can get over the wall. We'll need something to cover the top. It's got glass embedded in it. There are four doors to choose from. I saw servants using the far right one. They were carrying trays and I think that's our best way in."

"Okay. Let's get to the gaming house." Springheart led the way down the hill.

Willowvine did one more scan of Vitenkar's home. Finding nothing different, she followed. If they'd been seen, there would have been a change in someone's aura.

Any suspicion and there would be scree coming to get them.

Chapter 19

Their inability to fully see the scree's home was drilling a hole in Springheart's stomach. They never went in without knowing the danger. Willowvine's power allowed them to know the location of every person, even if they only knew the layout of the building. Now, they were not only planning on going into Vitenkar's home without knowledge, they were walking into a gaming house filled with scree.

Springheart needed to make sure Willowvine didn't go rushing through the crowd. They needed to be extra cautious to avoid bringing attention and raising suspicion.

The gambling house was dingy, and the only upkeep seemed to be strengthening the door. It would take a determined attack to get through if the owner wanted to keep someone out. The noise was deafening, and it explained the location. There were no homes nearby, only warehouses and storage buildings, no one to complain, no one to bring the gaming to an end.

"There's going to be more than just dice and cards inside," he said. "Try not to look too closely at the side rooms and dark corners."

These houses usually had some form of brutality going on for the patrons to bet on. If it were just pitting one man against the other, he would be surprised. And if it wasn't, Willowvine didn't need to see it.

"I'm coming in, though." Willowvine reached for the door to push it open.

Springheart pulled her hand back. "Follow me. Try to pretend I'm in control for now. I don't think they are used to women coming here. At least women who aren't serving them, or for sale."

She swallowed and paled a little. If she was scanning the auras now, he probably didn't need to warn her what was inside.

"I'd be surprised if Maynard came to such a place simply to gamble." Springheart wouldn't admit she'd been right, that Slack was up to something, but he no longer thought that the man was whiling away time. If this is what he did in his spare time, the guild would need to know. Couriers who were at risk of manipulation were no longer an asset.

Willowvine blinked and the fear left her eyes. "Fine, but maybe you were right. If he needed to get more information on one of the names on the list, it would explain why he'd come here." Her tone was gleeful rather than reasonable.

"Don't get careless. Now, is there anyone on the other side of the door?"

She closed her eyes and then a grimace twisted her face. "No. Everyone is farther in. But the emotions are... bad."

"Stay behind me." He gave the door a push. It swung open with little sound. The roar of voices almost overwhelming his senses, Springheart led the way into a wide common room. In the center, a wild cat was trying to defend itself from a large bird. Springheart had never seen a hawk so large. There was magic involved here. Someone was husbanding animals for this purpose.

There would be no way to carry on a conversation in the bedlam of encouragement to the animals. He scanned the crowd for Maynard's dark hair and height. The room contained mostly humans and scree. Maynard should have stood a head above the other humans, and his dark unbraided hair would make him different from the scree. There was no sign of him. There were alcoves in the far corner, but most of them were open to the room. The roar of the main event made anything else impossible.

He turned to take Willowvine outside.

She wasn't there.

His breath froze in his lungs. He should have made her stay outside. This place could hold any number of people who wanted an elf in their control. He would have to find her fast.

Slipping behind the crowd, Springheart found a path between the gamblers and the wall. No one paid him attention as he circled the room. The fighting in the pit was becoming more frenzied, and no one wanted to miss the kill.

His path took him past the alcoves, toward the only door he could see. The rooms were empty as expected and there were no stairs he could see up or down. This was not one of the sophisticated gaming houses. There was no place for a musician, no kitchen. People didn't come here for an evening's entertainment. They came to feel the excitement of raw risk.

His heart slowed its racing as he realized that there was no one covering the exit. He reached the door and inched it open. It led to an alley, blocked by three large humans sleeping off their night.

Whoever had taken Willowvine hadn't come this way.

He moved faster now, needing to get to the street. If someone had taken her out the front door, she could be on a ship within minutes. He tried to calm himself with the knowledge that she would have fought. That would slow down her captors.

He reached the final alcove, only steps to the door.

A hand grabbed his elbow and drew him inside before he could pull back.

"He's not here," Willowvine said, her breath hot on his ear. "He was talking to those two scree in an alcove across the way."

"Never do that again," he shouted back. "How do you know they were talking over this row?"

She pulled the curtain across the alcove and all sound stopped. "The curtains are warded. I didn't say I could hear them; I saw them as they closed their own curtains." Then she opened up the room again to see the crowd.

WILLOWVINE SAW the two scree she'd pointed out start to move toward the door. Whatever they had discussed with Maynard was more important than watching the end of the battle.

"Let's go." Springheart pushed her ahead of him.

They slipped through the door and Willowvine saw the scree turn at the mouth of the alley. "They are going home." This could be an opportunity.

"There's no way we can get information from them," Springheart whispered. "Maybe we can get a glance through the gate if we follow."

She nodded. There was more than a chance. She was going to see what the front of that house looked like. Going over the wall was just as dangerous from the front or the back. If they came in the front, they wouldn't have to use the servant's passages. She feared they would get trapped if that were their only route. She signaled Springheart to drop back so they didn't look obvious. He told her to be careful again, but slowed and let her get closer to the scree.

They reached the gate to Vitenkar's house without alerting

the scree that they were being followed. It helped that the day was busy and people hurried on errands. But if these scree were skilled, they would know she was there.

The scree banged on the gate and waited for it to be opened. Willowvine joined a small group of farmers who were pushing their barrows home now that the market had closed.

The gate opened and she stepped toward it, tripping the boy in front of her to make a commotion so she could slip inside. Even a moment's inattention would help.

Willowvine made it through the gate as it closed on the heels of the two scree. For a second she was able to see the entire front of the property. A large paved yard, a wide door, and no permanent guardroom.

A hand grabbed the back of her tunic, and she yelled for help. Springheart would find a way to extricate her from the situation. The scree who had captured her, pulled her back to the gate, but Willowvine kept her eyes on the building. Two stories, the top only covering the left half of the building, which was built in two wings and there were no windows on the right side. A warehouse. That's where they would start.

Her captor was about to toss her back onto the street as she'd hoped. Her relief was short lived. A scree stepped through the main door and stared at her. His hair was braided with bones and his smile was that of a hunter about to take his prey.

"Halt!"

"I was trying to find my lover," she whined. "I saw him come in here. Where is he? Why are all these scree here? What have you done with him?" It was a weak play, but she knew that Springheart could hear her. He'd find a way to save her. He'd be angry, but it was worth the risk to get the information they desperately needed.

"Call for the town guard," the scree who could only be

Vitenkar ordered. "Turn her to the wall and make sure she does not see anything more."

This was bad.

If he convinced the town guards to take her in, Springheart would have to waste time getting her out. Why didn't she listen to him? Whatever made him think through the risks was missing in her. Maybe it was a kind of magic? But if she'd taken the time to think, they wouldn't have her information. Of course, the information wouldn't help if she couldn't get it to Springheart or if he didn't act on it. Sometimes you just have to take the chance.

It only took a few minutes before she heard the stamp of town guard boots approaching. A few years ago, the town had been much more dangerous. The guard had learned the value in making noise to intimidate whoever they approached. If they came through the gate, the only way she would leave was in their custody.

The gate opened and Willowvine waited for the boots to approach. It didn't happen.

"Outside the gate," Vitenkar ordered. "No one comes inside."

She let out a breath. On the street there would be hope. Springheart would be there. And Vitenkar couldn't do anything to her in public.

THE GUARDS TOOK the elf from his warriors as soon as they were outside. Vitenkar looked at the crowd that was forming and called for five of his men to clear the area. Too many people watching would limit his options with this elf. That's why he'd called the guard. Either they would sanction his actions, a possibility if he paid well enough, or they would take her away and put her in the jail. If he acted on his desires, too many people would think his actions distasteful if they witnessed it — although he realized it would not be wise to bring attention by making her disappear.

He spun to search the street for a partner. No one was there, but he couldn't help feel that someone should be. He had her alone. He would make sure that she spent at least the night in the cells. Every night that he kept the Stone was precious. It would only take a few more nights before the world was changed in his favor forever.

"She was preparing to steal from me," he announced. The guard should take his word for what happened. He was a respected merchant, and she was an elf. Even to the human that must mean something.

One of the guards was a goblin and the other a human. The goblin knelt behind the girl, tying her hands together in a complicated knot that she wouldn't be able to release without a knife.

The human turned to Vitenkar, took his information, and then asked, "Do you have proof of her motivations?"

"There is no other reason she would enter my home."

The guard reached down and pulled the girl's head up by her hair. "Who are you?"

"I am innocent. My name is Butterflower."

The guard sighed and Vitenkar became worried. Why was this fool delaying taking the elf to the jail? "There is no innocent reason for her to be inside my walls." He itched to reach for her and shake the truth from her body.

The guard looked at her. "Why did you enter the grounds?"

"I saw my lover go in there last night. I thought he was in trouble."

The girl was smart. She didn't talk too much, didn't give anything for him to twist other than bare facts. "There are no elves on my property."

The guard ignored Vitenkar's comment. Keeping his attention on the girl, he asked, "Who is your lover?"

"He's human and married. I don't want to get him in trouble," she muttered. "Maybe I got it wrong. Maybe it was another gate. I'm sorry."

"She's lying," Vitenkar said. "There are no other houses like mine. She was intending to steal, and I want her taken to the jail. I will not feel safe unless I know she is locked up."

The guard looked over at the five scree who were keeping the street clear. "I doubt that you have reason to be afraid with these warriors on the premises."

"I insist that you take her into custody." Was the man looking for a bribe? If he was, then he should have taken Vitenkar aside. No one would offer a bribe in such a public space. The penalty was too harsh, and he didn't trust his warriors to be loyal if there was any accusation.

"If you have no proof, then I can't hold her without cause." The human guard motioned to the goblin who started to untie the knots. "Perhaps you should just make sure your gate is locked."

Vitenkar realized that the authorities would bring him no satisfaction. If he didn't find a way to have her arrested, she would be walking away and planning her next attack. He couldn't allow for the risk. If she wasn't going to jail, she'd have to be killed. "Very well, let her go. I'm sure that she will meet her fate eventually. Thieves don't live long."

He watched the girl tense as she took his meaning. The guard looked suspicious, but didn't say anything. When the girl was untied, she stood and started glancing for escape routes.

"Perhaps I can come to the guard house to report my lover missing." She stepped a little closer to the human guard. "I've caused enough problems here. I apologize. I was mistaken. Perhaps you can forgive my impetuous actions. I am in love."

Vitenkar didn't answer. He needed to get back to the warehouse to check on the Stone and if the guards took her away then he would be freed of the trouble of hiding her body. It occurred to him that there was a reason that her partner, and he was convinced there was a partner, was not coming to her aid. She was a distraction. While his warriors were here, and he was outside, another thief could be searching his home. His heart stopped, and then his breath caught.

Vitenkar looked at the scree warriors he'd called out. "Follow them and make sure she doesn't come back." Turning on his heel without acknowledging anyone, he shouted for the gate to be opened.

He would make sure she was no longer a threat, or set his warriors to patrol the yard.

Chapter 20

He would lock her in their rooms.

Willowvine seemed determined to kill him with her risk taking. She'd talked her way out of arrest, but now Vitenkar would be on his guard. They would still have to go into the house, but it would be infinitely more risky now that she'd caused such a scene.

On top of everything, she had to extricate herself from the guard without making matters worse. He couldn't trust her to do that, so he'd have to go get her.

Following the group to the guardhouse was easy. They were focused on Willowvine who was chattering on about her imaginary lover; a man who sounded more like Maynard Slack with every sentence. At least she knew how to use facts to support her lies. He hadn't needed to teach her that, she'd learned it from the orphan gang.

When they arrived at the guardhouse, Springheart waited until they got inside and then counted slowly to a hundred. He needed to make them think that someone had reported her to him. That he was summoned from elsewhere. He heard her voice as he approached the door. No one else was speaking. It meant he didn't have to interrupt anyone, especially a guard — they hated that.

He pushed his way into the foyer. Willowvine was standing at the counter, the five scree were lounging against the wall, and two guards were trying to take notes on her missing lover.

"Be quiet," he said with as much authority as he could throw into his voice. She stopped talking, glared at him, and then looked down. "You are right to be abashed. I heard what you have been doing. It is not acceptable."

"Who are you?" the human guard asked.

"I am a courier. My name is Springheart and this child is my apprentice. I will take her now." He moved to grab her arm, but the guard stepped between them.

"She is giving a statement. You can take her when she's finished."

"Oh, let me guess. She's reporting a friend missing? Or a human lover? Or a… I don't know what her latest fantasy is."

The guard looked at Willowvine and she started to tremble. "There's no lover?" he asked.

"No." Springheart reached for her again. "I will ensure she understands the consequences of her behavior. I would appreciate it if you didn't report it to the guild." He could feel the scree interest in the conversation as they stiffened out of their lax stances.

"I need to hear it from her," the guard insisted.

"I'm sorry. I won't do it again. Please don't get me kicked out of the guild." She sounded as though she was about to burst into sobs.

The guard looked away from her to assess Springheart. This was the point where they were ready to let him fix what she'd done. They didn't want to tangle with the guild. The guards relied on couriers too. He couldn't volunteer the information for fear it would sound forced. He needed the guard to ask what would happen to her. Springheart stepped toward

Willowvine. Making his voice harsh, he said, "This time I will not be so lenient. You have proven you cannot be trusted."

Her trembling increased and a sob broke out.

"What exactly are you going to do?" the guard asked.

Springheart let the question hang for a moment, as if he was considering what to say. "I can only be sure she is not causing trouble when she is locked up. She will have a day to consider her behavior before I let her see the outside of the basement. A day of darkness and hunger may do what a beating has not."

The guard stepped forward and placed a hand on Springheart's chest. "Take care that you do not overstep. She may be your apprentice, but you are subject to our laws. I know the elves work differently, I know the guild has its own ways, but this island is a civilized place. I do not expect to find her body left within my jurisdiction. Do you understand?"

Springheart looked around at their audience. Internally he was surprised that the human would protect an elf. Outwardly he needed to be indifferent to their cares. "I would not kill an apprentice for disobedience." He made it clear with his manner that he would kill for other reasons.

The guard took his hand off Springheart and stepped aside. He addressed the scree. "You will not attack these people. Return to your employer and do not bring our attention to you again."

Springheart gripped Willowvine's arm and forced her to rise. "We will leave you now."

As they entered the street, he whispered, "Stay frightened until the scree are out of sight."

They walked away, Willowvine acting cowed, but actually watching the scree as they strode away from the guardhouse. When they were alone, he let her arm go. "Let's hope the guards tell Vitenkar that you are locked up. You'll have to go disguised until tomorrow." He didn't want to get into an argument about her obeying him. That hadn't worked up to now, and he didn't need to waste his energy trying to make her be more careful. She just wasn't capable of it.

THEY WERE in the small room that had been reserved for them at the guildhall. Willowvine had been uncharacteristically silent the entire walk from the guardhouse to the guildhall. She wasn't sulking, she wasn't arguing, but she wasn't speaking. Springheart was too experienced to take that as a good sign.

"Okay, I guess you had a reason to go in there, and we fixed the problem. What happened?"

She took a sheet of blank paper. "Thanks for getting me out of the guardhouse. They didn't seem to want to let me go."

"That's a good thing. If you had just walked out of there, then Vitenkar would have stayed on full alert. At least now he might think he's safe for tonight."

"He has the Stone," she said, turning the paper toward him. "I saw the layout of his home. The warehouse is right there. He has an army surrounding him. He has it."

Springheart looked at the drawing. "We'll still have to go around the back."

"Yes, that's too bad. But you think he has it, right?"

She looked at him and he saw her need for his agreement. He couldn't validate her actions, but his caution wasn't sufficient to quell the hope rising as he checked the drawing. "I think so. But let's review what information we have before we go. There may be another reason that he needs an army." *Other than just the fact he's a scree.* "Did you see anything else?"

"Aren't you going to lecture me on the dangers of taking risks?" she asked. "I mean we can get that over with and then I can just do a full report."

He sat and started sorting through the papers he'd pulled from his bag, placing everything to do with Vitenkar on one pile. She was not going to deter him from a careful plan. "Has a lecture made a difference?"

"I do try, but I couldn't let an opportunity like that go by. If the fates want me to see something, I should look."

As much as he wanted to repeat all the lectures, he realized that she would never change. Her risk taking wasn't about being too young to understand the consequences. It was a part of her. "I've given up, Willowvine. We'll deal with it when this is over. We'll go somewhere and I'll teach you more about defense, and we'll find a way to help you see the consequences so you can be prepared. But I give up trying to stop you doing stupid things."

"Really?"

It seemed that she was eager to learn when it suited her. Maybe they'd been in the guild for too long, and he'd become complacent with that structure. They needed a break and maybe training would take her mind off this new elven guild idea. "Really. Now, what did you see?"

"There were about twenty scree in the courtyard, and I was able to sense about the same number of auras in the left wing of the building. We need to find a way to avoid them, but I can't imagine Vitenkar lets them roam his house at night."

He knew that there would be patrols, but she had a point. Vitenkar was unlikely to share his home with any of the warriors, even with something to guard. "What makes you think the Stone is in the warehouse?"

"If I were hiding something like that, I'd want it with me, or where people aren't around. So, my guess is that it's in his private rooms, or in the warehouse." She pointed to the drawing of the building. "Here, on top of the barracks, is where he sleeps, see the windows over the warehouse are dressed in heavy curtains. The warehouse is almost an add-on. There must be an internal entrance, or in the back. I couldn't see any doors in the front and the wall around the compound is right against the warehouse on that side."

"And why would he hide the Stone in the warehouse rather than his room? That's what you think right?"

"Yes. His private rooms are too obvious. And we probably won't be able to search them anyway. The warehouse can be left empty, especially if there's only one way in or out, and the room is probably full of crates and boxes."

"So the Stone won't stand out," he finished for her.

It did feel right, and if that was all they would get, feelings, they needed to follow up. That put them in a difficult position. Maynard couldn't be with them, couldn't be hanging around in secret either. There was no way to avoid breaking the Heart Oath if they were this close. "We need to get rid of Maynard tonight."

Willowvine grinned. "How are we getting in?"

And there she was forgetting about anything but the one facet of the danger.

"First, how are we going to keep Maynard busy?" He wasn't going to lecture her, but he'd find a way to teach her to look at the whole picture, so she'd have a better chance of survival.

Before she could answer, Maynard slipped through the door to their room.

Chapter 21

Willowvine was convinced that Maynard Slack knew something.

When he'd found reasons to cross all but two buildings off the list to search leaving only Vitenkar's home and a nearby warehouse, they'd tried to get him to follow up on the gaming house, or to write up a report for the guild board. He'd found a way to dodge both suggestions. That's when she knew that it was a lost cause. He clung to them offering all the help in the world in that creepy, oily way he had.

They'd had to give up trying to put him off.

Now they were on the street with the stupid man in tow pretending they would search the warehouse. He still didn't know where they were actually going, but that would change at the next intersection. She'd agreed to keep quiet and let Springheart figure out a plan on the walk. He was good at that and, despite the fact she'd never admit it, she was terrible at it.

"Maynard," Springheart said as they reached the corner. "You need to stand lookout." He tipped his head in the direction of the warehouse on Wharf Street she'd been watching yesterday. "Can you find a way to hide and still be able to cover any approaches?"

Willowvine schooled her expression. She knew that they were going to slip away, but they needed Maynard to be sure they were there long enough for them to enter and exit the warehouse, get to Vitenkar's home, search it, and get back into the warehouse. That was a long time and if Maynard decided they were taking too long, he might come looking.

They approached the now empty cafe. The tables chained to posts, chairs having been taken inside leaving little cover, but Maynard nodded. "I'll be at the right angle if I get behind the tables. There's just enough room."

Springheart checked the position and gave his approval. "You'll be fine for a few hours. We should be done well before the sun comes up, but if not, make your getaway and wait for us in the guildhall."

Willowvine saw some emotion cross Maynard's face. She expected annoyance at being treated like a trainee. Without her ability to read his aura, she couldn't be sure, but she thought he was amused. "What signal should he use?" she asked. Breaking her agreement to be silent in her impatience to start. It was going to be tight to get through this before dawn.

Maynard imitated a gull. "I'll do that three times. It is common enough not to turn casual interest into suspicion, and loud enough to reach you no matter where you are in the building."

If the man weren't so creepy, he'd make a great partner.

They waited until he was settled before hurrying across the road into the shadow of the warehouse.

THE DIVERSION HADN'T TAKEN as long as she feared. Springheart had wasted no time on elaborate measures. As soon as they entered the building, he'd pulled her through a back door and they'd raced around the city to the back of Vitenkar's home.

Now they were waiting as the servants settled. The rest of the building was quiet, lights only showing in the top windows — Vitenkar's private rooms. Barracks were hidden behind the kitchen and servant's quarters, but a quick scan revealed that there were only ten scree there, and most were sleeping. If she was right, Willowvine was confident they would be back with Maynard before he became suspicious. Despite a lurking doubt deep in her mind that her inability to read Maynard's aura was a sign that her talent was waning, she told Springheart to enter.

"When we get in there, no side trips," Springheart cautioned. "We are going to the warehouse first."

"I know, but if it's not there, I want to take a peek at the rest of the house."

Springheart tapped her shoulder and pointed. "Time to go."

She noticed the light from the oven had gone from bright orange to a warm glow. It was banked for the night. She scanned the auras and reported, "The barracks are quiet. One person upstairs, probably Vitenkar. I sense a couple of people in the front yard. No one is feeling worried, let alone on alert."

Springheart told her to lead, so Willowvine crouched low and ran to the deep shadows near the servant's door. She felt Springheart join her, and then used her picks to open the lock. They slipped inside without incident. Springheart tucked a wedge of thin wood under the door to stop it swinging open. The door would seem secure to a casual check.

When he was done, Willowvine ran to the top of the stairs, stepping on the edges of the treads to avoid squeaks. The doorway at the top was covered with a heavy curtain. Willowvine smiled, so many people traded security for a little quiet. The occasional slammed door near her bedroom would never make her do that. Any servant could lurk behind a curtain obtaining useful information or paying off a debt by giving access to thieves. It worked for their purposes; a curtain allowed her to peek out discreetly in both directions — another reason she would never use one. A cracked open door was only helpful in one direction, and it couldn't be hidden.

They were lucky, the upper hall was empty. One lantern at the top of the stairs gave as many shadows as it illuminated. Each end of the hall terminated in a solid door. To the left was the room where Vitenkar's aura still remained calm; to the right, an empty room. If the Stone wasn't in the warehouse, it could be in the empty room.

She let the curtain sway back into place and turned to Springheart. "We can get downstairs. There's no one in the hall, right now, but I'm not sure that will last. You go first, I'll keep scanning auras until we are inside the warehouse."

Springheart slipped around her and through the curtain, reaching back to give her the okay. Dropping into a light trance, she followed. He would ensure she didn't stumble. She didn't trust their luck to continue, but they made it to the warehouse door with no incident. The incident waited for them at the door. It was locked and the mechanism was built to resist easy picking.

She signaled Springheart to cover her and reached for the lock. If anyone came out into the hall, they would see her, and she couldn't scan auras while she worked the picks.

Speed will not help.

She slid the wrench pick into the hole. The lock was a dual version. She clicked the tumblers into place for the first set, twisted the picks and went back through the tumblers on the second sequence.

The occasional shout from the barracks raised her nerves beyond the level where she could keep her hands steady. She had to stop working the lock and poise to run until convinced they were still safe. By the time she twisted the picks and felt the lock open, she was sweating. This was new for her; every entry up to now had been smooth and fast.

Pushing the door open, she reached for Springheart. When they were inside, door closed but not locked, she let out a breath and pushed the tension from her body.

"It needs to be locked," Springheart whispered. "If he checks it, we can't have it open. And the noise of him unlocking will give us time to hide."

It was their only way out.

She knew he was right, but it felt like she was locking them in a prison, a dark, silent prison. Willowvine felt for a latch, but there was none. She'd have to lock it with the picks by feel because they couldn't risk a light this close to the door.

She felt Springheart's presence move away while she worked. As the lock reset, Willowvine heard the dry scratch of a flint and then a dim light came from a lantern he held.

Willowvine strode calmly toward the glow, feeling her emotions settle as she put distance between herself and the door. She put aside the creeping terror of knowing they would have to leave without being sure no one was waiting.

"It's big, and crowded," Springheart said. "We need to split up."

Willowvine looked around as her eyes adjusted to the dimness. There were racks filled with crates. If they had to open each one, they would be here a week, and they didn't have that time. "So, a quick survey first? Maybe the Stone is sitting in the open."

Springheart chuckled. Handing her a second lantern, he pointed to the racks on the right. "Start there and scout the five rows to the center. I'll do the same from the back. We'll meet here and figure out the next steps. Be fast, we only have about an hour before we need to leave or Maynard will think we're in trouble."

Willowvine raced along the racks. All the crates looked the

same. The labels ranged from kitchen tools to jewelry. Taking a moment to prise open one at the far end of the first rack, she confirmed the contents matched the label.

Joining Springheart, she reported, "There are a few odd boxes in the far corner, but we'll need time and tools to get them open. They are all big enough to hold the Stone."

He glanced up and said, "I found a vent in the ceiling. We can get back in through there. We'll need ropes. What kind of tools?"

"A crowbar and a hammer, and something to muffle the hammer." Willowvine wanted to try the crates, but she knew they didn't have time. If they found the Stone, they would still have to reseal the crate so Vitenkar wouldn't know. "Then we come back tomorrow night," she said.

Springheart nodded but didn't say anything. She felt a thrill of pride that he didn't argue about her suggestion. He must think she'd made the right plan.

DID THEY THINK HIM STUPID? Maynard watched the two elves disappear behind the closing door of the warehouse before slipping out of his hiding place. Brushing the dirt from his clothes, he stretched out the kink in his back that had developed in the few minutes he'd been crouched in the shadows of the tables.

They were going to the house Willowvine had stumbled into earlier. The one that had gotten her arrested. The fool. He wasn't going to wait here like a lackey. No. He would be there waiting when they came out. Maynard Slack to the rescue if he was right about their inability to fool the scree.

He strode the streets with confidence, knowing the attitude could do more to avoid trouble than any weapon. He considered how to find the elves, it would not do to have them slip past him and then complain that he wasn't in place when they exited the building they were supposed to be searching.

The elves were likely to be heading for the rear of the scree building. That's where he would have gone. The front was far too occupied for them to slip in unnoticed. One thing they couldn't know was that the majority of the warriors were in the gaming house. Perhaps if they had that information, they would be using the front gate. Then again, perhaps it would make them careless to think they had fooled all of the warriors. It would give him a chance to take whatever they had found. A voice inside whispered that the elves were never careless. The girl might be reckless, but Springheart was a cautious one.

As he arrived at the hills behind the compound where the scree lived and conducted business, he saw two slim shadows at the servant's entrance one crouched in a stance that screamed lock picking to his experienced eyes. It was good to have confirmation even though he had no doubt where they were headed. Maynard settled down, back against a tree, ready for a long wait.

SPRINGHEART WAITED while Willowvine scanned the lobby for auras. She'd shown progress in learning caution with her plan to come back when they had what they needed.

"It hasn't changed," she said, reaching for her picks. "The barracks is still almost empty, and Vitenkar is still happily doing something in his room."

He nodded for her to use her picks, dousing the first lantern while he waited. The risk of light bleeding outside was low compared to the risk of taking too long to get outside the room.

A tiny click announced her success.

He touched her elbow to make sure she waited for him. He signaled that he would go first before dousing the second lantern. Willowvine pulled open the door just wide enough for him to slip through. The hall was empty. He reached back and touched her wrist before slipping aside to crouch in the shadow of a table. He was only immediately visible now from the top of the stairs.

In seconds, she had the door relocked and was beside him. This was the point when they were in the most danger. If Vitenkar decided to check on his troops, or his inventory, they had nowhere to go. He tapped her knee to get Willowvine moving up the stairs and to the left of a decorative table near their exit point. When she was settled, Springheart raced to join her. Halfway up, someone banged on the front door. He kept moving, hiding beside Willowvine just as the door to Vitenkar's quarters opened.

"Who is disturbing my rest?" the scree roared.

A door banged open downstairs followed by a scuffle of feet. Vitenkar continued to march toward the noise.

"While they are focused on the front, we'll go through," Springheart whispered to Willowvine. "You first."

"No. You go first, I'm smaller and faster. I can sneak better." She elbowed him to stop his argument.

It frustrated him that there was no time to make her do as he suggested, but she would hear from him as soon as it was safe. The sound of the front door opening, spurred him through the curtain and down the stairs. She would be on his heels. He slipped through the rear door holding it open for Willowvine. They still had time to lock it and avoid rousing suspicion.

She didn't come.

Swearing, Springheart entered and ran back, hearing a shout and a pounding of feet on the grand stairs. He glanced through the curtain to see Willowvine sprawled on the floor. His anger drowned in a wave of fear. He reached for her hand, but she pulled it away.

"You need to go. I'm caught. Figure out how to get me out of jail."

No one had seen him, so he ducked back into the stairwell and sped to escape. He didn't bother to lock the door; it would only take time and they knew the security had been breached. He cut across the bottom of the hill and melted into the shadows.

Rounding the side of the scree's home he was just in time to see the guard drag Willowvine through the gate, Vitenkar shouting orders as they headed toward the town guardhouse. When they passed his hiding place, Springheart slipped from the shadow, walking along the street innocently. A citizen wondering what was causing the disturbance so late at night.

At the first cross street, he saw movement in a doorway. A figure stepped out of the shadow. Springheart realized it was Maynard, lurking rather than keeping lookout. Springheart flicked his fingers to indicate Maynard should join him.

"What happened?" he asked under the cover of Willowvine's protests. "I heard noise and came to see if it was headed toward the warehouse."

Springheart didn't challenge the clear lie and didn't explain why they were outside a completely different target. "Someone called the guard."

Could it have been Maynard? Springheart pushed away the thought. Maynard had no reason to sabotage them.

"What gave you away?"

Springheart glanced at Maynard and then pulled him into a doorway across from the guardhouse. Willowvine continued to argue and struggle against the grip of the two guards as they pulled her into the station. "There was nothing. Someone guessed, or it is a disastrous coincidence." He didn't believe in coincidences, and the guards had shown up too late for someone who'd seen them enter.

"An oddly timed coincidence," Maynard said. "Why were you there?"

"We found a tip," Springheart said.

He wasn't going to explain their actions when they needed to find a way to free Willowvine. And to get back into Vitenkar's warehouse. There was no longer any doubt in his mind that the Stone was there. It was just a matter of getting enough time to search properly.

Chapter 22

Springheart was outside. Willowvine knew it. He just needed time to find a way to get her released. She'd never live it down; only kids tripped over loose rugs. All she could think of to explain it was she'd become complacent because there were so few scree in the house. So when the guards arrived, she was startled into stupidity.

Now it was time to try to talk her way out of the charges. "I don't know why he was so mad. The scree invited me in for a drink." She didn't expect them to believe her, just to sow some seeds of doubt. If Springheart was close enough to hear, he might be able to use the lie. "He said he was sorry to make such a fuss this afternoon."

One guard tied her hands then the others stood behind her to stop Willowvine from trying to run.

The head guard was a different man than before. At least that was in her favor. She couldn't get the guild involved by identifying herself as a courier this time. There was no doubt that she was going to be arrested unless a miracle occurred.

The man looked down at her from his perch and tsked as he placed a blank form on the counter. "Your name?"

"But I wasn't doing anything wrong."

He dipped his pen in a pot of ink "That's up to the judge. Name?"

They'd come up with fake names and Springheart would be using it to get her released. That way nothing tainted the reputation of the courier guild. "Butterflower."

She watched as he scratched the name in the first box on the form, adding the word elf after.

"Address?"

"I'm between residences," she muttered the words to give them a little veracity. "I was hoping I could bunk in the scree's house for a while. Who called you anyway? He seemed surprised that you came."

The head guard scribbled *homeless* in the address box and then sighed. "Now tell me the story from your side." He settled back in a listening pose.

"I just did, why don't you just let me go?" This stalling wasn't getting her anywhere. If Springheart didn't come soon to rescue her, then she was going to spend some time in a cell. There was no way she could talk her way out of this situation.

"You were found in a citizen's house. He claims you were stealing." The head guard looked her over one more time, signed the form, and then put it aside. "Put her in the first cell. We can keep an eye on her."

"Why does his word count more than mine?" Willowvine pleaded as she was shoved toward the doorway leading to the cells. Knowing it was inevitable didn't help now that she could smell the sourness emanating from the darkness.

Springheart had better find a solution to this problem soon. If it came down to a choice between the Stone and her, he'd have to take the Stone. Either she'd be free in a couple of hours, or she could be here until after the full moon had risen and the elves were doomed or saved.

. . .

THE GIRL MUST HAVE IT, Maynard thought. They wouldn't be delaying the contract to get her out if they'd missed it. "Do you have a plan?"

He looked at Springheart. The elf was watching the doorway, seeming to ignore the growing foot traffic. The scree were done with the gambling distraction, and not all were heading home. A few taverns would get a boost in business before all the warriors were in barracks.

"It's going to take some powerful leverage to get her free, and she can't spend too long in there. We need her." Springheart looked toward the center of town.

The fool was going to ask the guild for help. That would work for Maynard because getting the guild involved with the guard would drop the two elves down a few points in the ranking. It just seemed too easy. "Maybe Lisseline would be the best choice. She has good relations with the guard and the mayor." He could probably manipulate her better than most of the others as well.

Springheart turned to him. "Are you insane? Bringing the guild in will only make it worse."

Too easy all right. Maynard bit back a retort and said, "We can try bribery."

"We don't know how many people are involved, and we don't have enough money for many. Vitenkar will be able to buy more loyalty than we can, anyway. He has fear on his side as well as money."

Maynard moved to match Springheart's pace as the elf marched away from the safety of the shadows. "Maybe we can let her stay there until the scree is no longer interested. We can bribe a lower level guard in a couple of days. We must have money for that left in the expenses."

The Stone wasn't on the girl, there was no way she could

have hidden it in a pocket. If it was that small, they wouldn't have had time to find it before capture. And she'd had no time to hide it before the guards caught her. Even if they didn't have it, they knew where it was. He'd bet his reputation on that. "The scree won't deal with this until the morning. It would make him look bad to have been vulnerable enough to let a child in his home. Or worried enough about such an event."

Springheart turned a corner before answering, "He's probably turning his household upside down try to figure out what she stole. And stop referring to her as a child."

Suddenly realizing where they were going, Maynard came to a halt and grabbed Springheart's arm. The elf shook him off but came to a stop. Maynard drew them into the shadows. "You can't be serious. The guild board will dismiss you for contacting the client." No matter what he'd overheard in the guildhall, Maynard knew that client courier meetings were restricted to instructions, and delivery. Both meetings were held in the guildhall, most of the time with a board member present.

Springheart leaned in to answer quietly, "This is a special contract. I have to talk to Devissial."

SPRINGHEART WALKED along the path to Devissial's house. He wished he could think of an excuse that would send Maynard on his way, but the man was there to help, so Springheart turned his thoughts to what he needed to say to Devissial. "This must be discreet as well as fast," he said. "Let me do the talking."

"Of course," Maynard agreed. "Far be it from me to interfere."

Taking a chance on Maynard being unwilling to break guild custom, Springheart said, "If you want to leave me here, I'm happy to do this alone. If you go now, then the guild won't have any issue with you going to a client. It'll all be on me."

Maynard reached for the door knocker. "You said it was a special case, so let's get the girl out of jail. We'll worry about what the guild thinks of your decision when the contract is complete."

A human servant answered their knock and ushered them into a small receiving room. Springheart glanced at the furnishings, trying to get a feel for the man who owned them. There were few decorations, the walls were plastered white, the furnishings dark wood with deep red cushions. The atmosphere welcoming, and clearly expensive. Devissial wasn't shy about displaying his wealth, but did so with taste. Without Willowvine's ability, he would have to read the man's emotions the mundane way.

The servant returned with three glasses of wine on a sliver tray. "Mister Devissial will be here shortly. Is there anything I can bring you?"

Springheart thanked him as Maynard opened his mouth to ask for something. They would not be in Devissial's debt for anything other than information. Maynard would have to keep quiet. Perhaps he would be better at it than Willowvine. As soon as the thought entered his mind, Springheart felt shame. He had to stop thinking about her negative traits as her only traits. In fact, those traits had been of use, so perhaps they were not always negative.

The servant nodded and departed as quietly as he'd entered. Sitting in one of the chairs Springheart waited until they were alone before saying, "We aren't here for a visit."

Maynard took a glass and leaned against the wall. "I know, but I'm hungry. I thought elves were civilized."

Springheart refused to respond. Why Maynard Slack was suddenly insolent was unexplainable. Whatever had caused it he wasn't going to feed the mood.

"What can I do to help?" Devissial asked as he entered.

The man looked polished as if it was midday rather than the early hours.

Springheart told him the details, as much as he could share in front of Maynard. "We need your help to get Willowvine free before morning."

Devissial looked to Maynard who seemed to take the attention as permission to speak. "I'm sure it was not her fault, sir. The girl is competent."

The tone of Maynard's words made it clear that he didn't think that at all.

Devissial raised an eyebrow. "I know that. She would not be on this job otherwise. Why are you here?"

Springheart stepped in before Maynard could take offense and make matters worse. "The guild has provided us with Maynard's time to ensure we are able to use our efforts to the critical tasks. He is not aware of any details. Now, will you provide the funds for a bribe?"

Devissial smiled, placed his glass on the table, and said, "Better, I will use my influence. That way we do not need to waste time finding the right person to bribe. Let us go now. The girl will leave with us. I can guarantee that."

Springheart glanced at Maynard as they exited the room. He seemed calm now. Perhaps the rebuke would keep him from interrupting again.

A few minutes later they entered the guard station and Devissial pointed his companions to the chairs lining the far wall. "Let me do this. Don't argue or react to what I say."

Springheart watched as his client marched up to the desk where a guard was rising, having just noticed the man approaching.

"Citizen Devissial, what brings you here at this hour?" He spoke with respect.

"I am here to retrieve my servant. The hour was determined by your actions." Devissial seemed to grow in stature as he talked.

The guard licked his lips. His voice shaky, he asked, "Which servant?"

Springheart froze as his heart stopped in fear that Devissial would use her real name.

"An elven girl. How many of them do you have in your custody?"

Springheart quietly took in a breath as he admired the man's ability to avoid any details.

"She was found inside a private home."

"Where is her accuser?"

The guard swallowed. It didn't seem like he was happy that Vitenkar was taking his time. "He said he will come as soon as he is sure what she stole."

Devissial leaned toward the guard who shrank away. "More likely he is preparing false evidence. The child is naive, but not a thief. I will take her home."

Springheart watched the guard as he clearly considered arguing. He pitied him. The man was trying very hard to do his job in the face of political expediency. Eventually the political aspects won out. "I'll have her brought out."

They waited only a few minutes before Willowvine strode into the room, a second guard right behind. She smiled at them, until Springheart narrowed his eyes to signal her to be more humble. The desk guard pulled a form from a folder and handed it to Devissial who looked at it with contempt and crumpled it before dropping it to the floor.

"Thank you for your cooperation. Now, we will go home, child. You will tell me what really happened when we are there."

Chapter 23

Devissial left them outside the guard station. Willowvine knew they had used him to free her, but could wait for the details until Maynard left. They still had time to retrieve the Stone if they went back right now. But that meant Maynard had to be gone.

"We need to let the guild know what happened," she said into the silence of the dark street. "If they hear about it from anyone else, we'll have to explain away the interpretations." As much as she wanted to be free of the guild, she didn't want to be ejected. The anonymity that the guild provided was precious. The wards the guild had around their doors were not the usual ones. The guild wards clouded the minds of anyone trying to figure out which of the people entering were clients and which were couriers.

She was certain that the only reason she was freed so early was that the guards didn't know that she was a courier. If they had, they wouldn't have listened to her story at all. She would probably have been left in the house for Vitenkar to deal with. Or turned over to the marshal depending on the views of the guard in charge.

"We don't have time," Springheart said. "We can't wait until the guild board convenes."

Willowvine watched Maynard consider her statement, his gaze on the ground. If she was right, he was now torn between staying with them and taking the opportunity to bad mouth them to the board members. She'd thought about this while sitting in the cell. He had always been competitive with them, and he'd wormed his way into the contract as their agent. He wanted to be the number one courier. If he agreed, Maynard would be gone at least a couple of hours. The trick was to make it his idea.

"If you don't think it's important..." she let the words trail off giving Maynard an opening.

He took the bait. "The girl is right," he said. "We cannot let them hear about this from anyone else. Devissial may already be composing the message."

"We need to prepare for our next search," Springheart said.

Maynard straightened. "I'll take care of the board. Shall we meet for breakfast and discuss our plans?"

That agreed, Willowvine watched Maynard head toward the guildhall. "We have time, right?" She tugged at Springheart's arm. "I wasn't in there too long?"

He shook off her grip and started walking toward their rooms. "What tripped you?"

"The stupid rug. I can't believe I tripped over the rug. One second I was right behind you, the next my hands hit the ground."

"Will you be tripping later?"

Springheart was angry with her.

"No." She grabbed his arm. "What do you want to say to me?" They couldn't enter that house again with hardness between them.

"I need you to be ready for surprises. If you get caught

again, it won't be so easy to get you free." He held open the door to their rooming house.

"You are angry because I tripped?" Willowvine tried to stop the fight she felt from showing in her voice. It wasn't her fault, but there wasn't time to talk him around.

"I'm not angry. It scared me when you fell. I don't want to lose you."

They were inside their room now. It was a safe place to talk. Willowvine opened the chest they shared for storing tools and mementos. It hadn't occurred to her that Springheart would be afraid. *He should have more confidence in me.* "I'll be careful," she said tying off the coil of rope they'd need to get in through the vent. "I'm sorry I scared you."

Springheart handed her the hammer and screwdriver, and then slipped the crowbar into his own sack. "I know. Look, Vitenkar has had time to move the Stone, but not enough to have moved it far. We can be fast because there's no one to dodge. We're not going to search the house if the Stone isn't in the warehouse."

"But—" she stopped herself from finishing the sentence.

Springheart tucked another rope into his pack. "We still have time enough for Vitenkar to get careless again."

She thought that Vitenkar would be more vigilant as time passed, not more relaxed, but didn't argue.

THE BULK of his army was settled in their beds, but Vitenkar didn't care. They should have been there earlier. Wherever they were, they would regret leaving him unprotected. It could have ruined his plans. With only a few warriors around, the damn elf had the run of the house. He was sure that she hadn't found the Stone. It was too well hidden, and too big for her to have concealed on her person. Anyway, she was in a cell now and would be there until morning.

Time to make sure that his warriors were more alert from now on. The battles wouldn't be too far away and warriors who were lazy or distracted would not help him win control of the world.

He marched into the barracks, expecting the men to come to attention. No one moved. He scanned the room for Dintral or Ballian. Dintral was unfortunate enough to be curled up on the floor asleep. Vitenkar brought his lieutenant to his feet with a kick to the ribs, then snarled, "Get their attention."

It took far too long to get the men to rise. Most were weaving on their feet as they stood, drunk. He was wasting his money. If there were any other way, any other mercenaries available, he'd have these fools out on the street before they were sober. But there were no others to hire.

"We were attacked tonight," he shouted. "It was not successful because even at reduced numbers the scree always triumph."

Rather than a roar of victory all that Vitenkar heard was a loud belch.

"Our time is nearing. To ensure that we are ready, no one will be absent from this house. Sober up. Tomorrow you will all be in training until you are too weary to drink. Anyone who disobeys will learn what punishment means in my army."

A few groans responded.

He turned to Dintral. "Find Ballian and relay what I said. If any of the men are unable to train at dawn, the two of you will receive the same punishment as they do."

He didn't wait for a response, simply turned and marched from the room.

In the main hall, Vitenkar took a moment to calm himself. He had no doubt that the warriors would perform when needed. It was in the nature of the scree to fight, not to lay waiting for the fight. It would probably have been a better tactic to keep them occupied for the last few weeks. He would make sure that they had no time to waste between now and the first battle.

He turned to go back to his bed, but something seemed to be pulling him back. Spinning to face the door to the warehouse, his confidence drained away. He told himself that there was no way the girl had entered the warehouse, but the question kept appearing in his mind — was there? Did the elves have a way to break the unbreakable lock?

Sighing at his doubt, Vitenkar pulled the key from his pocket and went into the warehouse. Lighting the torch set beside the door, he looked for clues that someone had been there. No footprints, but that was simply because there was no dust. He supervised the cleaning of the warehouse to ensure no dust or other contaminants infiltrated his crates.

Vitenkar made his way to the far corner of the warehouse to where the Stone of Family resided in its crate. Despite the fact that it was still crated and there was no evidence of tampering, Vitenkar knew he had to move it, or he'd fret all night.

He knew that the warehouse was still the safest place for the Stone, but if in the unlikely event that the elf had entered, there were other places to hide the crate without taking it from the room. He hooked his fingers through the space in the slats and effortlessly lifted the small square crate. Walking the length of the row of racks, Vitenkar stopped at the end, this was actually the farthest place from the only door. If it sat here, against the back wall in this far corner, it would blend in with the other oddities of all different sizes and weights.

Vitenkar placed the torch in the bracket on the wall to free his hands. Moving a crate aside, he slipped the one containing the Stone behind it. He stepped back and looked at the arrangement from a couple of angles, finally deciding it looked fine in the light from the torch. Thieves, elf, or other species,

wouldn't dare to have a bright torch lit when they were here —
no. Not when, if.

He brushed his hands together in satisfaction, grabbed the
torch and made his way out of the warehouse. A glass of
brandy would help calm him enough to sleep until morning
when he would deal with the elf girl.

Chapter 24

The roof was easy, at least for an elf. Springheart's gaze searched the hills behind Vitenkar's house, but there was nothing to cause concern. After a quick scan, Willowvine reported that the barracks were full of auras, sleeping, or drunk. One aura was in Vitenkar's room feeling satisfied. There was nothing in the warehouse below them. If Vitenkar hadn't removed the Stone, they were almost done.

He bent to check their entrance. The vent had a cover like a large hat, intended to discourage birds from nesting. It was attached with four screws that Springheart removed quickly. Lifting the cover, he looked into the room below.

"It's too far to just drop," he said to Willowvine.

She grunted a response and took the end of one rope and tied on a grappling hook. He scanned for observers in the hills as she knelt at the edge of the roof and tucked the claws of the hook under the eaves. It wouldn't have held a human, or most other species, but it was a sufficient anchor for an elf.

"Okay, I'll go first," she said, returning to his side. "Should I light a lantern?"

Springheart looked around again. The stars and moon

were still in the sky. "No, we'll be fine for a few feet inside. No need to take the chance someone will notice the light. Go."

He checked the line as she dropped. It ran smooth, and she was down in a moment. He saw her step aside before giving the rope a tug to let him know it was clear. He tossed the two sacks of equipment to her and slid down. Feeling hopeful that the whole job would go as well as the entrance, he nodded at her to run to where they suspected the Stone was stored.

Suspected was probably not the right word, he hoped it was there. If it wasn't, they were stuck with no clues to follow.

The crates all seemed to be in place. Willowvine was already prising the lid off the first one. Springheart lit a lantern and placed it away from any straw that might escape. He watched as she carefully pushed aside packing material to reveal wine glasses. A quick feel to the bottom of the crate and she confirmed they were the only contents.

"Damn," she whispered. "I had a good feeling about this crate."

Springheart hid his smile. She was still young enough to think feelings could help. The only help they could use was tracking magic and neither had that. "I'll close this one, you open the next."

It took longer than he expected, but soon they were replacing the lid on the last likely crate. They'd found glasses, wooden toys, flatware, mugs, and ceramic figures. No stones.

He hit the last nails in and placed the crate exactly where they had found it. While Willowvine repacked their tools, he studied the area. Having no other clues made him reluctant to give up on the location. From where he stood, it looked like crates filled the space, they had been very careful to replace the each one they moved so no one would suspect that anything has been touched.

"What now?" Willowvine interrupted his unproductive observation.

He turned to her. "If you were Vitenkar what would you have done after the guard left?"

"A scree would probably go beat someone up," she responded before closing her eyes. "You mean as someone who had an object as powerful as the Stone regardless of species."

He didn't bother answering her comment. This was something he needed her to think through without prompting.

After a few moments, she said, "I would move it. I tried to think of some other action, but nothing else makes sense."

"We were only gone about an hour, so he couldn't have moved it far." Hope was creeping in to vanquish the defeat.

"It's still here," they said at the same time.

Willowvine scaled the rack and looked in from above. "There's a space." She returned to his side. "We're looking for a rectangular crate about this big." She held her hands apart about the length and width of a loaf of bread.

"I think we're in the right row, otherwise he's taken it closer to the door," he said. *Or he's taken it to his quarters.* That was a problem for another night. They only had time to search this row before the sun rose. Morning would tip off anyone who entered because there would be too much light. They would only be able to continue searching if Vitenkar was ignorant of the weakness in his security. He lit a second lantern and handed it to her. "You run along the top. I'll take the middle and bottom. Wait for me under the vent."

Willowvine scrambled to the top shelf and started moving along the racks, her eyes focused on the crates beneath her feet. Springheart, much slower, bent to check the density of the crates on each row. There was no place where one was tucked behind another. The inventory seemed normally arranged, each container close enough to the other to ensure maximum storage space, but far enough apart to be easily removed from its place.

He approached the end of the rack before looking up from

the bottom row to see Willowvine sitting cross-legged on the floor, the snuffed lantern beside her, the rope hanging behind her, a shaft of moonlight gilding her hair. Her focus was on the object cradled in her legs — a small crate that could have held a loaf of bread.

Abandoning his search, he rushed to her, crowbar ready. Within moments they were looking at The Stone of Family.

WILLOWVINE STARED at the Stone in her lap, disappointed that it was nothing special. There were words on the bottom. At least she thought it was the bottom. There were traces of dirt and a few stains on that side. Other than that, there was nothing else to separate it from any other paver on the streets outside.

Springheart passed her the sack they'd brought to transport it. "I'll put the crate back together. You pack our things. Be fast. I don't want to have anything happen now we have it."

Within seconds, their packs were ready, Springheart handed her the now empty crate to replace. He slung their two sacks over his shoulder, handing her the one with the Stone. She stood at the bottom of the rope waiting for him to clear the vent before starting her own climb. Halfway up, she heard the door open.

"Assemble the army on the hills. I will be there to lead the training in a few minutes," Vitenkar said to someone before shutting the doors.

She froze. If he was headed directly for the Stone, they would have only a few seconds to re-attach the vent hood. Without that, he would know someone had been there. He'd have a party of warriors on them before they could make their escape.

It is not the time to panic.

She shimmied up the last few feet and drew the rope

behind. Springheart hadn't heard any of the action. Willowvine grabbed the vent hood from him and placed it over the hole hoping that it wouldn't blow off before they could secure it.

With the hood in place, she felt safe enough to whisper the facts to Springheart. "I think we'll be facing his warriors any second."

"Go down and wait for me two streets away in the direction of home," he ordered. "I'll secure this and meet you."

She wanted to say they should stay together but knew that the Stone was the most important thing. They needed to get to Devissial to find out where to deliver it.

The hills were still clear of scree, but false dawn was lighting the sky, taking away the advantage of dark. She bent to remove the grappling hook before climbing to the ground. She heard noise building inside the house as she melted into the shadows and crept toward the street.

Waiting in a doorway for Springheart to join her, Willowvine felt time drag on. Shadows evaporated in the rising sun as she started counting to measure the delay. Reaching one thousand, she began to think of plans to rescue him. Relief replaced anxiety when he strode around the corner to join her.

"Keep walking," he said as he passed.

When she was beside him, Springheart continued, "We need to hide it before we go to Devissial for instructions. I do not want to chance anyone stopping us and stealing or confiscating the Stone."

Willowvine agreed. She'd had plenty of time to think about what powerful leverage the Stone was to the right people. "When we do finish the contact, can we please get something more than a handful of money?" They hadn't had a choice with sealing the gate. The deed had been completed before anyone thought of payment. This time they could hold the

Stone, not for ransom, and not to destroy the elves obviously, but to get the exile lifted. That might be enough.

Springheart stopped, looked around, and then led her down a path to the right, not directly to their rooms, and not toward anything she knew as a hiding place.

"What would be enough, Willowvine?" His words were calm, no tone of argument for her to push against.

"Lifting the exile?" She hoped he wouldn't have a logical answer, and wished that she'd thought more about the idea.

"It would be good to go home once in a while." This time she heard an echo of her own desire for the elven lands.

"It will be easier to get them to accept orphans if we are living amongst them." Maybe she could get the elven courier guild started too. It was almost the same as what Springheart had been doing before exile.

"How do you intend to get them to agree?"

Now she heard the trap in his voice. He wasn't agreeing with her, he was getting ready to show her how stupid her idea was, and how easily he could demolish her logic. She had to admit that she usually lost the battle because she hadn't thought it through. One day she'd find the time to do it and he'd be surprised. "We can hold the Stone until they agree?" She hadn't meant it to come out as a question.

"You would destroy the elves just to get revenge?" He led her around another corner, heading toward the docks.

The street was starting to fill with early risers. Servants heading to the market square to be there as soon as the farmers set up, clerks heading for businesses to open the doors before their employers arrived, fishermen carrying buckets of the night's catch for sale.

Willowvine stepped closer to Springheart so they could keep talking. "No, of course not."

"Then how are you going to use it as your bargaining chip?"

"They don't need to know that I won't." It had sounded better in her mind than it did spoken.

Springheart drew her into the entrance of an alley. He placed his hands on her shoulders and made her look at him before he spoke, "They won't bargain. If they believe you would destroy the elves, they will not allow you back onto the elven lands. This need you have to be accepted will cause you only pain."

"It's not fair," she said. "We're not a danger to them. Why won't they tell us what is so wrong about being an orphan?"

He sighed and let go of her shoulders. "I don't know. It is a question you can ask, but do not go forward with this plan. Simply ask. Do not bargain. If I could find a way to help you get over it I would, but you must deal with it."

She swallowed the bitterness of the truth. "How did you get over it?"

He smiled. "What makes you think I am? Perhaps I'm simply better at schooling my emotional responses."

Chapter 25

This will be over soon, Springheart thought. When it is, we can get back to normal.

Finding a hiding place was turning out to be more difficult than he expected. Taking the Stone to the guild, or home was too predictable and despite precautions, it could be stolen back. The docks were promising because they had no affiliation there.

"So, where are we going?" Willowvine asked. "It only needs to be hidden for a couple of hours at most, right?"

"That's the best case," he said.

The docks were getting busier, and now that they were away from Vitenkar's house and the fear of pursuit, he realized they needed food. The stone would be safe and they could explore options over caf and pastries. He led Willowvine to a cafe where the outside tables were mostly empty, and they would have privacy. When she was settled, he placed their order.

"We need somewhere that no one will connect to us," he said when their food was delivered. "One we can get to at any time."

She devoured a pastry before asking, "I guess it's too risky to put it in a safe at the money lenders?"

"Yes, and it would be suspicious if we only left it for a few hours." He looked around. The wharf stretched out from the end of the street. There were two other cafes and a general store. A new building was going up a few doors away. A convenient pile of rubble set in the street. It would be unfortunate to find their Stone embedded in a new wall if they left it there.

"Do you think Vitenkar will search for anything involving an elf?" Willowvine asked. "Or two elves?"

Good question. "If he's training his warriors, we have a couple of hours before he will even look for the crate. Unless he did that right away."

"He would have been looking already, and we would have heard the ruckus," she said with the confidence of youth.

"He thinks you are still locked up, and he won't know about me, Maynard, or Devissial until he checks there." Springheart didn't want to get careless, but it didn't seem risky to think they had three hours to get the directions for the next step and be on their way. "What are you thinking?"

She leaned forward. "Rent a room for a couple of days even if we only need it for a couple of hours. Find a loose board or something to hide the Stone." She took the last pastry. "If you do it, then he'll be delayed even if he searches for a connection to me."

Springheart thought through the consequences of her plan, aware that they were eating into the leeway they'd just discussed. No plan was going to be without danger, and he decided that renting a room was less risky than dithering around for a better one.

"I'll be back." He took the sack containing the Stone from her and crossed to the closest inn. It was named Sailor's Haven and was the less seedy of the two choices.

A quick transaction bought him the keys to a room with a

bed, small table, and wood-burning stove. Sailors always needed a hidey-hole, so chances were good that he'd find a hiding place.

Locking the door, he checked the floorboards — all firmly nailed in place. The stove was filled with ashes, which would cover the Stone, but leave him dusted in the grey residue. A tentative tap on the wallboards revealed a loose slat under the small window. Popping it open, he tucked the Stone inside and replaced the slat. Wishing he had a ward to add to the protections, Springheart left the room, pocketing the key.

Willowvine was waiting with their packs over her shoulder. "We need to go," she said.

He followed her away from the docks, waiting for her to explain the urgency.

They turned a corner before she spoke again, "Maynard saw me. He doesn't think I noticed. He went along the wharf and I don't think he could have seen you leave Sailor's Haven, but I lost track of him in the crowd."

Chapter 26

Vitenkar stormed through his gate. The gate guard greeted him and was rewarded with a snarled response.

They had released the girl.

It was even harder to believe they would not tell him the reason. Worse still, she had been free long enough to return to his home. The guard hadn't even thought to inform him. The Stone was in danger. His plans were in danger.

Continuing to his room, Vitenkar retrieved the warehouse key from his safe and charged down the stairs to the door. He stopped before unlocking it. If the Stone were gone, he would need to move fast. Turning to march into the barracks, he roared, "Find Ballian and Dintral. Send them to wait outside my room." A second thought pushed at his rage. "Gather in the courtyard. Await instructions."

It took only a few seconds for the warriors to respond, a few seconds longer than it should have. If he were right about his prize, there would be generous punishments handed out later. Random and brutal punishment would be the best way to keep them alert and trying to please.

Anger cooled a little, he strode to the warehouse door, slid the key in the lock, and opened the door. Inside, door relocked, he sniffed the air, was it different? Should he have checked earlier when he came to retrieve the delivery for that fool customer?

"The past cannot be changed," he muttered as he raced to the hiding place. Pulling the front crate down, allowing it to drop without caring about the contents, Vitenkar stared at the small crate sitting where he'd left it.

Hope bloomed. No one would have taken the time to remove the Stone from its crate and put it back together. He wanted to believe the warehouse was impenetrable. The law ensured that his inventory was safe. Stealing any of his goods would cost the thief months or years of their life. But the Stone wasn't merchandise. He couldn't declare ownership.

Hand trembling with fear, he reached for the crate. Taking a deep breath, he lifted.

It was too light.

The Stone was gone.

He smashed the crate against the wall with a roar, cutting his hand on the splinters created with the violence of his action.

Racing back to the door he struggled to unlock it with shaking hands. He stepped through to see warriors running to the courtyard. At least they now obeyed his orders without argument. He locked the door again because the merchandise still needed protecting even if the Stone was gone. Then Vitenkar marched to his chamber to see if his lieutenants were as changed as the warriors.

Both stood to attention facing the door. Something in their steady gaze heartened Vitenkar, made him feel like he had a household army like the noble scree.

"The elven girl must be found," he said with no preamble. If they were obedient, then they would not need to know why.

"Alive?" Dintral asked.

"Yes. Alive and able to speak."

Ballian relaxed from his stance. Vitenkar braced himself for insolence. This lieutenant was smart and that could be an asset or a failing depending on how he used it.

The man spoke respectfully. "You want the warriors to search the city? Are you prepared for the repercussions of the violence they are going to perpetrate?"

"The girl must be found and fast." A little explanation might help them to succeed. "She has taken something important."

"It's a small town, but there are many places to hide. Do you want the warriors to demolish buildings? Do you want to have to answer for their actions?"

His fury subsiding, Vitenkar started to realize that his emotional reaction was bound to cause more problems. He'd promoted these two for a reason, so perhaps listening was not a sign of weakness. "What do you suggest?"

Ballian relaxed more. The lack of respect conveyed would have brought him sever punishment in any other situation, but Vitenkar was so desperate to act that he allowed the liberty.

"I presume you don't wish us to know what she stole." He waited for Vitenkar's nod. "You don't want anyone knowing that something is missing?"

The girl could be boarding a ship for the mainland, or the resting place of the Stone. If it left the island, he wouldn't be able to find it again. "Yes, stop asking questions and tell me what you suggest."

"I needed some information to formulate my suggestion," Ballian said then paused as though thinking. Just as Vitenkar was about to order him to speak, he continued, "We should be more discreet. A few of us, the more experienced, can search without tipping her off, or attracting attention. We can take her somewhere that you can question her without exposing this incident to anyone."

Vitenkar smiled. The man was a genius at this. Keeping her away from his home gave him more options. Killing the child here would mean he'd have to dispose of the body. When he had his treasure back in his hands, he would kill her. "When you find her, gather her possessions and inform me of the location."

Ballian looked at Dintral and then said, "A reward for this would help to motivate the searchers."

Money. Everyone wanted money. When had the scree lost the value of honor, obedience, and victory? "Yes. See to it." He tossed a small bag of coins to Ballian and dismissed them.

Chapter 27

Whatever they had been doing at the docks was finished, Maynard thought as he stepped out from behind a stack of crates that sat ready to be loaded on a ship. The girl couldn't have seen him, or the two elves would have come looking as soon as Springheart exited that inn.

The guild had taken his report without question and dismissed him. It rankled that his efforts weren't recognized as they should be. He smiled at the thought of the board members' contrition when he saved the contract. The short meeting was a benefit this time, because he was free to rejoin Springheart and Willowvine. He would find out what Spring-heart was doing in Sailor's Haven and he would not let them fob him off with a menial task again.

Maynard hurried so he could catch them far enough from the docks to avoid suspicion, but close enough not to lose them in the streets winding into town. A dash down a side alley allowed him to call out as they passed the entrance to a cross street. "Good morning. Are we ready to continue with the contract?"

The two elves came to an abrupt stop and then beckoned

him out to the crowded street. Springheart answered the greeting with no enthusiasm. "Are you rested? Did you make the report?"

Caught off guard, Maynard answered truthfully. "No rest, as I'm sure you can understand. The guild did not say anything, I'm sure they will ask for a full debrief when the job is done. Where are we going now?" Given the direction they were moving, Maynard feared they were going to the client's house. If that was true, then they had the Stone.

"We need to do this alone, Maynard," Springheart stated. "It comes too close to the secret than is prudent to share."

Damn! They had succeeded.

"At least allow me to escort you, to wait until you are finished, and rejoin the contract. Surely you will need more assistance." He imbued as much meek sincerity into the words as he could.

Springheart scowled and glanced at Willowvine. She shrugged and didn't offer any suggestions. The fact that they didn't want him around wasn't new, but it was vital that he didn't let them dismiss him.

Finally, the elf said, "Do not try to enter the client's home. Wait for us on the street. If you are not there, we will not waste time looking for you."

He nodded and thought better of answering. He had what he wanted. No need to talk his way out of it.

Chapter 28

Devissial's home was exactly what Willowvine remembered it to be. Humans liked to display their wealth, like it was evidence of winning a game of some sort. Granted, this display was more tasteful than most, but still far too many rooms, and far too many objects with no use but decoration. They were left waiting in a different room than before. It was furnished with a few lushly colored sofas, a delicate table, and hundreds of books. What kind of man needed an entire room for a library? And she recalled the number of books in the first room. The man must be a scholar.

"Don't talk about the arrest," Springheart said. "We don't need any delays. We want the instructions, and then we can be on our way."

She rolled her eyes. He thought she'd embarrass him with her thanks to Devissial. Well she would thank him, but only after they had their instructions. "Can I speak at all?"

He chuckled. "You can do all the talking if you like. Just keep to business."

Willowvine almost said that she would let him lead the meeting but thought better of it. If they were going to start a new guild, she needed to learn how to talk to people like Devissial. "Okay." Springheart wouldn't let her get into trouble.

The client only kept them waiting for a short time. When he entered, he waved them to the sofas. "Refreshments?"

Willowvine smiled. "We do not wish to take any more of your time than necessary. We have the object and will leave you to your business as soon as you provide our instructions." She wondered if that had been too brusque. Didn't people of this stature generally want a little flattery?

Devissial gave a small bow. "I will need some proof first."

Her worries set aside by his graciousness, Willowvine glanced at Springheart. He gave her no clue, so turning back to the client, Willowvine said, "We don't have it with us." Why was he suddenly being so suspicious? They didn't have time to sit around and chat.

"I would not know if it was real by looking at it. I have three questions. If you have the object, you will be able to answer."

That worried her. They hadn't studied the Stone. What if they missed something important, something that was an answer? There would be more delay going and checking the Stone and returning. More risk too. Springheart would not appreciate that. Trying to sound as confident as the marshal did with clients, she said. "What are the questions?"

Devissial held up one finger. "Does the object belong in the earth, air, or water?"

That, at least, was easy. "The earth."

He held up a second finger. "How old is the object?"

That gave her pause. The Stone was as old as the world, but had it always been The Stone of Family? She closed her eyes. There was nothing in her memory to tell her how old the writing was, or if the writing was a spell, or a label. "As old as the world," she said, deciding that was the only answer she had any sense of confidence in.

It seemed she'd guessed right because Devissial nodded. "There is a message on the back. What does it say?"

She'd seen the writing but hadn't read it. If they hadn't been interrupted maybe they would have looked. Frustrated, she was about to say they would have to come back, when she realized that Springheart might have read it. She turned to him and asked, "Did you have time?"

He nodded at her with a smile that told her she'd passed some test. Perhaps he meant her to overcome her need to do things by herself and realize that asking for help wasn't a failure.

He stepped forward. "The message reads, one for family, two for all elves, three for abundance. Please do not ask what it means." Springheart stepped behind her to let Willowvine take control back.

Devissial laughed. "I would not expect you to understand an elven message in less than a year of study. Wait here."

While Devissial was gone, Willowvine took the opportunity to question Springheart, "If you knew, why did you make me ask?"

Springheart drew her to the window at the back of the room. It faced a garden that was tightly controlled in flowerbeds of various colors that probably displayed a pattern from the upper floor balconies. "I was not sure that you didn't know. And there is value in thinking, perhaps as much value as in doing or speaking. What did you learn?"

Her answer was forestalled by Devissial's return. "This envelope contains your next instructions. Please confirm that the seal is unbroken."

Willowvine checked the seal on the back of the envelope. The wax was deep purple, a color of importance, and warded so that it could not be resealed once broken. "It's not been tampered with."

"You must open it and read it here. When you have done

that, you must burn it." Devissial handed her a flint. "Place it in that box when you have lit it. When the fire is out, close the box and shake the contents so they cannot be reconstituted."

'That box' was a sliver tobacco case sitting on the delicate table.

He bowed and left them alone again.

Springheart motioned for her to break the seal. In the envelope was a single sheet of paper with two lines of writing.

Now that you have the object, you must place it in the center of the labyrinth on Crous Isle. Do so by the full moon's rise and the elves will survive. Fail and your people will wither away. You will contact Leafcreek when you arrive to receive the details of the ceremony. He will act as witness to your actions.

Willowvine reread the message on the chance that there were other meanings, but it was direct, oddly so for an elven message. "It's like they don't think of us as elves," she said, feeling cold and abandoned as if the exile were fresh, not five years old.

Springheart took the message and the envelope, placed them in the silver box, flicked the flint and watched the flames devour the message.

"They don't. At least this burning will stop Slack from getting his hands on the message."

Chapter 29

As they exited Devissial's home, Springheart saw Maynard Slack waiting for them on the street outside. He suppressed a sigh. Once again, they needed to find the man a task that would keep him out of their way. Something that would take long enough for them to retrieve the Stone, and book two passages to Crous Isle. Once they were aboard ship, the man would no longer be able to interfere, and the oath would be under less threat of being broken. Their lives would only be hostage to this contract for a few more days.

Willowvine stepped ahead of him, apparently still taking the lead. "We will need supplies for a long trek across island. Can you manage that?"

She reached toward Springheart, hand out for money. He placed the purse in her palm, trusting her to keep back enough funds for their passage and expenses. Willowvine spilled a few coins into her hand and passed the pouch back. "This should be enough. Bring everything to our room at the guild, we'll meet you there before dinner."

Maynard took the coins, automatically verifying the amount. "What will you be doing?"

His question was clumsy. Springheart was sure it was a reaction to Willowvine's commanding attitude. Taking a little pity on the man, Springheart answered, "Nothing that we can disclose to you. The supplies are important. We do not have time to do both. I see the value of your help now. I apologize for the way we have treated you."

Let that confuse him.

Maynard looked from the money to the two elves, clearly trying to form an argument, but not able to do so. "Very well, is it supplies for three?" he asked.

Let him think he was still joining them, Springheart thought. "Yes, but we will go on foot. The cost of animals is too high."

Still clearly trying to ask a question he couldn't formulate, Maynard finally nodded and walked away in the direction of the market.

When the man was out of sight, Springheart felt confident enough to urge Willowvine forward. "The Stone first. Then we will find a way to leave the island."

She hurried toward Sailor's Haven, turning only to say, "I think we missed the tide. Will we be able to hide on the ship until sailing?"

"I don't know, but we can ask." Springheart slowed and reached for Willowvine to draw her close.

There were scree about. Traveling in pairs, they were entering a shop on the next street. "I think he's noticed that we took the Stone."

They blended in with a family of farmers who were pushing empty barrows away from the market. Boisterous after a profitable morning, the group happily provided room for two elves to travel in their midst.

When they were ahead of the scree, he drew Willowvine to the side. "I don't know how many of them are on the street. It's not like scree to ask questions quietly, so I think only a few. We need to split up and meet at Sailor's Haven."

"Be careful," she said. "They are probably looking for me, but we don't know that. They might be just looking for elves. Don't wait long for me, if I don't meet you there, I'll find you." She didn't wait for him to answer.

Springheart watched as she scrambled up the side of the building to run the roofs. He had time to do more than just hurry to the inn because she would have to find places to cross the radiating layout of the streets. They needed to know the extent of the search and the layout of the town would work in his favor. A quick glance over his shoulder showed the two scree were leaving the building. Using the alley, he sped to the next main street over. Watching for a few minutes, he saw no scree, so he slipped to the next thoroughfare — no scree.

To be sure, he needed to backtrack and check the four streets on the other side, but time was passing, and he needed to move on. Knowing that there were no bands of scree marching toward the docks would have to be enough. Springheart abandoned his search and made his way to the inn.

Willowvine walked through the door seconds after Springheart. They were alone, so if the scree asked about an elven girl, no one would know she was here. Leading the way to the room he unlocked the door. The room had not been disturbed.

"Can you disguise yourself?" he asked as he removed the Stone from its hiding place, checking it carefully for any damage.

"How's this?" Willowvine asked.

He turned around to see a dirty faced human boy. She'd used the ash in the stove to darken the front of her hair and tucked the rest in the hood of her cloak. The ash also grimed her face enough to blur out the delicate features of elven heritage into the rough ones of a human child.

"Good. Keep your eyes sharp, we need to get passage to Crous."

"What about Maynard?"

He chuckled. "I think you frightened him. But he might be down here getting the supplies. We'll watch for him too."

HE WAS RIGHT.

The elves had sent him on an imaginary errand. They were seeking a ship.

Maynard stepped from the doorway of the cafe across the street from the elves. They hadn't seen him, so he felt safe drifting with the crowds that filled the wharf. If they thought he was cowed by the arrogance of the girl, he would use that. He would follow them, or better still take that object from them.

The girl was well camouflaged. He'd almost missed her. Only the fact that he knew they were a pair tipped him off that the boy was really an elven girl.

As he moved forward, he felt someone touch his arm. Spinning, ready to fend off an attack, he faced a pair of scree standing behind him. Scree always looked ready for a fight, bones braided into their hair, sword slung across their backs, it was disconcerting to see them outside the mayhem of battle or gaming.

"We are seeking someone," the scree on the right said. "Have you seen an elf girl?"

So, he was not the only one looking for them.

"Yes," he answered. "She was leaving town for the hills."

The scree turned to his companion, then back to Maynard. "We need to be sure that it is the right elf. Can you describe her?"

As if a scree could tell one elf from another. Maynard closed his eyes as though he was trying to remember what he'd seen. "Long white blond hair, she's short like an elf, maybe late teens." Opening his eyes, he stared at the scree. He needed them to go after the trail he was setting. It would get too complicated if he had to race the scree to the Stone. "There are only a few elves in town. How many young females do you think there are?"

Both scree bristled at his tone but held their anger in check. Interesting that Vitenkar was able to keep them on a leash. "When did you see her go?"

He thought for a moment. It had to be enough time that allowed her to steal the Stone and be far enough on her journey to lead the search party out of his way. And he was in danger of losing the real trail with this delay. His desire to look toward where he'd last seen the elves was fighting with his need to distract the scree.

"Just after dawn," he said. "You know elves. They love to spend time with nature. She's probably just gone for a few days in the trees."

The two scree were looking at each other now. Maynard willed them to believe him and go.

"Thank you," the same scree said uncharacteristically politely and then marched away. It was almost as disturbing as being threatened.

Maynard turned away from them to continue his search. Neither Springheart nor Willowvine were in sight. Heart racing in unexpected panic, he scanned the wharf. They must have entered a ship.

The only thing he could do was keep moving toward the end of the line of ships. No matter if they were buying passage, the ships had less than an hour before the tide turned and those leaving on this tide were busy filling their cargo holds. Last minute passengers would only be considered right before sailing.

Dodging sailors, and merchants, and sightseers, he kept

scanning the people ahead of him, not worried about being seen himself because he could give a story to cover his presence. As Maynard neared the end of the wharf, the noise became louder with sailors calling orders and directions in preparation for getting underway, the noise and the crowds making it difficult to focus on his targets.

Maynard came to a stop, leaning against a bollard. This running around was not productive. There was enough activity to allow him to stay hidden and observe. It took only a few seconds for him to see them. Walking down the gangway of a ship closer to town. The fools didn't know the procedure for sailing. On this tide the ships docked at the far end of the line would be leaving. The ones closer to town would go on the next tide..

They were talking and not paying attention to the people around them except the minimum required to avoid being knocked over. He couldn't let them leave. This might be his only chance. The crowds would give him cover and delay their pursuit.

Maynard launched himself off the bollard and ran the distance to the pair of elves. No one was bothered by the sight of another person running along the busy line of ships. He kept his eyes on the sack clutched at Springheart's side. Reaching to push the elf over with one hand and grab the sack with the other, Maynard took the prize and kept running.

There were a few shouts, but little sound of pursuit as he veered at the end of the wharf and headed toward the far road. He knew of an empty building that he could use as shelter. A place where he could confirm that he had the Stone. Somewhere he could decide on his next steps. He faltered as he realized that he had no idea where the Stone needed to go other than off island.

He heard footsteps coming and dodged into an alley, still heading for the hiding place. Off island! It dawned on him that he knew it was an elven artifact. Of course, he could deliver it to the elves. They could afford a generous reward. And he still had the money that Willowvine gave him. It would cover passage and a few days' short supplies.

The footsteps followed him down the alley. He tried not to look back, knowing it might mean the difference between escape and capture. The footfalls were too heavy for it to be the elves. Them he wouldn't hear coming. As he turned the next corner, he chanced a look. His pursuer was a human, one who was unused to running because he was red faced and gasping, and, more important, losing ground.

Chapter 30

"He went here," Willowvine said as she followed the gasping human around the corner into the alley. Following someone who was following their target was not the best way to get the Stone back. If the human lost Maynard, they were lost.

In the middle of the alley, her fears came true. The human was struggling for breath, he was at a complete stop, and Maynard was nowhere in sight. Springheart grabbed her arm and stopped her from running past.

"We need information," he said when she struggled to free herself. "It's Maynard. There are few places for him to hide."

The fat human would not be ready to speak soon enough. "If we wait…" She would lose her leverage and the elves would lose their future.

The man shook his head and pointed to the end of the alley, twisting his wrist to show that Maynard had run to the right. She didn't stop to wonder why the man was helping. She raced to the corner, feeling Springheart match her pace. They turned onto the street, weaving to avoid collision with a clerk carrying a stack of papers.

Springheart swerved to the other side of the man. "In

there, the broken wall." He pointed her toward the building site she'd noticed while waiting for Springheart to return from hiding the Stone only this morning.

"See you in there," she said, sprinting to jump the wall. Maynard had trapped himself if he'd entered the building. When they found him and she had her hands on him she'd make Maynard explain, then hurt him badly. Maybe she wouldn't wait for the explanation.

She glanced at Springheart before entering through the gaping hole in the front door. He was circling the small yard. It fronted the house and wrapped around the sides for a few feet. Between them they would find the thief and get their Stone back.

Inside there was enough light to see that the room was empty. The builders had stripped the entire floor of contents, leaving only one wall between the front room and what was likely the kitchen. A ladder reached to the second floor, replacing the demolished staircase. Willowvine hurried to check the back room, careful to look for attack before crossing the threshold. Nothing.

Her confidence waning as the seconds passed without finding Maynard, she ran up the ladder and checked each of the four rooms with no success. A glance through the back window showed her a narrow lane that butted up against the tall stone wall of the neighboring building. Swearing, Willowvine stood on the sill grasping the edge of the frame to lean out and scan the length of the lane.

It ended in another tall wall two houses farther up. The other end opened into a cross street at the docks. She hopped into the room and rushed outside where Springheart waited for her.

"I think he's gone back to the docks," she said. "Do you think there's any chance he is taking it to Crous?"

Springheart started running for the street. "I'd say no, but I didn't think there was a way for him to know about the Stone."

Their speed was restrained by the traffic on the street and Willowvine felt panic start to take over her determination. Maynard could be on his way to anywhere. "He wouldn't steal it if he was going to place it back in the right location. Why bother?"

They were at the docks before Springheart answered. "Money, power, something important to him."

Ships were preparing to sail.

"Money means he'll ransom it."

"Like you were planning?" Springheart asked sidestepping a line of men waiting for their wares to be loaded on a large ship.

"No, but if he knows it's elven, would he go to the elves?"

Springheart came to a stop. "You're right. How did Maynard know so much?" Willowvine saw the color drain from Springheart's face. "You remember that aura you sensed? When we were meeting with Devissial in the guild hall?"

Willowvine did, and she remembered how it had felt, muddy. "He knows what the tone is."

SPRINGHEART RAN TOWARD THE DOCKS. They didn't have time to think through the repercussions of their knowledge. Two ships ahead of where they stood, Springheart saw Maynard hand a heavy bag to the ship's captain before running up the gangway. Two sailors ran down and started undoing the ropes holding the ship to its berth. In the time it took Springheart to take a few steps forward, the captain was up the gangway, the sailors behind him drawing the ropes onto the ship. In seconds the ship had drifted far enough from the dock to be unreachable. As it cleared the berth, Springheart could see that all the ships anchored ahead of it were gone, the wharf empty to its end. Spinning on his heel he saw that the boats behind were quiet now. Maynard had taken the last boat for this tide.

"We can find out where it's headed," Willowvine said. "He doesn't know what we are supposed to be doing with it. We read the message and destroyed it."

Springheart couldn't take heart from what she said. If Maynard had found a way to listen in before, he could have learned the contents of the message. She was right about finding the destination. One of these ships might be persuaded to try a late sailing. With enough incentive, they could be on Maynard's trail before he was able to slip away. "Let's see if we can find some information from this captain." He gestured toward the closest ship.

They convinced the sailor at the top of the gangway that they were not a danger to the cargo by slipping him a few coins from their dwindling advance. While Willowvine kept her eyes turned to the horizon, Springheart questioned the sailor.

"I missed meeting a friend before sailing," he said. "Do you know where the last ship was bound?"

The sailor shifted position slightly as the ship rocked. "You don't know where you friend was going?"

Well, Springheart thought, I'd probably have been suspicious of easy information. "Perhaps friend isn't the right word." He slipped another coin into his hand and showed it to the sailor. "Can I rely on your discretion?"

Licking his lips, the sailor nodded.

"The boy and I were hired to retrieve the man. He stole a valuable artifact from our client, and left his daughter dishonored."

The sailor snorted. "Well, I guess if you can't get the honor back, a treasure might be worth it. The ship is called The Gull's Wing. Does a circuit between The City and here. Be back in three days."

Springheart saw Willowvine switch her attention away from the horizon to the sailor. She knew better than to speak. One word would destroy the illusion that she was a human boy. She glanced at the opening in the deck as if to say they should buy passage.

"Where are you bound?"

The sailor made an adjustment to the rope holding the ship to the wharf as the retreating tide brought them lower. "The City, a run to Crous, then back. You want passage on The Land Ho you need to see the captain."

If there were a pattern to the sailings, this ship would be the first out.

"Can I see him now?"

"He's on shore. Won't be back for couple hours." The man's gaze flicked to the coin, a signal that he felt that he'd given value and wanted payment.

"When do you sail?" Springheart didn't want to leave until he had enough information to plan how to catch Maynard Slack, and what to do about informing the client and the guild.

The sailor held out his hand, not willing to speak until he had his reward. Placing the coin on his palm, Springheart repeated the question.

Looking over his shoulder as if expecting punishment for sharing secrets, the man said, "Four hours until the first safe sailing."

He thanked the sailor and shepherded Willowvine onto shore. They had time. He wished they didn't, but that didn't mean they would waste it.

Chapter 31

"What do you mean she can't be found?" Vitenkar roared. "Are you suggesting she sprouted wings and flew away? She's an elf, not a fay."

Ballian seemed content to let Dintral take the full force of Vitenkar's wrath. He had to admit it felt good to shout at a man who flinched from his ire rather than one who would be unmoved.

"We had one tip that she'd headed for the hills. We have two warriors headed in that direction." Dintral responded.

Vitenkar doubted the tip was true. "She had help. Go to the town guard station and find out who got her released." He dismissed Dintral. When they were alone, he turned to Ballian. "You have an opinion?"

"Not so much an opinion as a feeling, sir. Going to the hills is not an escape. Eventually she would be found. I feel as though we've seen her, but not noticed her."

Why can't anyone speak plainly?

"Magic?"

Ballian firmed his lips as though sealing them against a dangerous response. When he finally spoke, it was in a tone that was so patronizing that Vitenkar had to battle to control his urge to smash the man's face.

"A disguise. It wouldn't take much to make her appear to be a goblin, a head covering and padding, a little dirt to darken her skin."

Vitenkar laughed. "She'd stand out more as a goblin on this island than as an elf. Don't be stupid man."

Stifling a sigh that made Vitenkar want to stab him in the gut, Ballian said, "True, but not if she were made up to pass as a human child."

His instinct was to dismiss the idea, but Vitenkar realized that his instincts hadn't served him well in this. A moment's thought and he accepted that it would be a perfect disguise. Not only would it fool anyone looking for an elf female, but there were too many human children on the island to check them all. Ballian had a point. "What do you think happened?"

The lieutenant shrugged. "If she were a scree, I'd say she got off island. I don't know what an elf will do to avoid notice."

The man's help was limited. Vitenkar told him to wait until they learned who was helping the girl and sent him back to the barracks.

If there were a spell that could help predict the actions of another, it would be in the book he kept locked behind the bottles of brandy and wine. He had most of the variety of chalks scree needed to release their magic. It was mostly for attack or slaying others, but it was possible there was something more subtle — and there was nothing else to do.

Placing the book on the table he started flipping pages. About three quarters of the way through he found a chalk and chant combination that would reveal where a particular thing or person was located. It would help. If she wasn't on a trail in the hills, perhaps they would recognize her surroundings and that would be an advantage.

Looking down the list of ingredients he saw that his stocks held all but one type of chalk; Visian chalk, deep blue and very rare, and the only one he needed for the spell. Rage at another disappointment took control. He kicked savagely at the table upending it. The book landed on the floor, on top of the broken wine bottle and pool of red wine.

Vitenkar trembled with rage that he couldn't burn out. A roaring in his ears blocked out sound as he struggled to reign in his fury. Minutes, or hours, passed while he was fighting the urge to storm into the barracks and tear off the head of the first warrior he found.

Someone banging on his door finally created a path for his sanity to follow.

"Sir, we have information." Dintral's voice came through the door.

Relief that it had not been hours, Vitenkar turned the lock. "Report."

"The town guards were approached by someone powerful; they would not tell me who, or whether that person was an elf or a human." Dintral paused. A flash of concern crossed his features. "The human matched the description of the man who told us she'd left for the hills. I cannot be sure if it was the same person or not."

The rage he'd barely gotten under control fled as though someone had doused him in an icy lake. "Where was this?"

"At the town guard house, sir," Dintral said uncertainly. "Where you sent me."

Vitenkar saw Ballian suppress a smile. Was the man amused at his counterpart's stupidity? "I meant where were you when the human lied?"

"Near the docks," Dintral confirmed. "He was headed to the wharf."

Vitenkar swore, and then took a bag of coins from a

drawer. "Find out if they left and where they are going. If they haven't sailed, bribe every captain to deny them passage."

Ballian took the coin and hefted it. "The tide has turned. If no one saw them board one of the ships that sailed, we have four hours, plenty of time to find them if they are here. Not too much time lost if we need to catch up."

Chapter 32

"We need to get on that ship," Willowvine said. Her frustration at the delays had her wound so tight she jumped at every sound. Even she knew enough caution to realize that this much tension would guarantee mistakes. "Waiting here isn't going to make that happen. What if we miss the captain? What if someone else gets the last passage?"

Springheart pulled her away from the window. After leaving the ship, they'd gone back to their room and gathered their belongings, all their coin, and two short swords. Then they had hidden in the building site, keeping watch for the scree.

Willowvine could see that he was as much on edge as she was.

"It has only been an hour. We have time. We'll leave soon," he said.

Soon wasn't good enough. "We could wait by the ship. We can't even see it from here."

If they missed this tide, Maynard would be too far ahead of them to catch. Even if they found his trail as soon as they docked in The City, he'd have a day on them, not just four hours.

"As soon as it gets dark, we'll go and find a better place to hide. The scree might still be looking for you." Springheart pulled a chunk of travel bread from his package. "Eat. We might not feel like it on board."

He was reminding her of how hard the passage to the island had been on her. It had been a day of hanging her head over the side of the ship, wanting to die. The memory didn't help her get hold of her emotions. She took the food and chewed it hoping that it would calm her. "Will we go together?"

He chewed his own hunk of bread, considering the question. "Your disguise will work better at night. Maybe we'll have to split up later, but we can stick together at first. If we get passage right away, we might be able to hide aboard until it sails."

She yearned to be able to wash the muck off her face. As soon as their ship was far enough away from Lands Home, she would do just that. "I don't like just waiting." The admission surprised her, until this moment she'd done what he'd asked. Every job until now had been a new lesson to learn, or an opportunity to hone skills she'd gained. Now that she thought about it, this whole job had been more of a partnership than any other. Springheart trusted her.

He shifted to watch the street from his place below the second-floor window. They were up there because it had the back exit. If someone came, they could be out of the window and halfway to the docks before the intruder reached the top of the ladder.

"You don't need to wait much longer," he whispered. "It will be dark enough soon."

As his words died, Springheart jerked away from the

opening and held up his hand to warn her to be quiet. Willowvine strained to hear what he'd noticed.

There were two people talking outside the garden. She peeped through the window and held still.

Scree.

They were splitting the contents of a pouch. Even when their palms were full, the pouch still clinked as the closest one returned it to his belt.

"You start at the far end," the lead scree said. "Don't over-pay, but make sure no one takes passage for the elf, or that human if he hasn't already left."

"If I run out of money?"

"Don't pocket any until we're done. I'll make sure we get our share before we hand it back to the boss."

The second scree shoved the coins into his own pouch. "He won't guess?"

The first scree laughed. "He may be a good merchant, but he doesn't know anything about warfare. If he thought we could do this cheap, he wouldn't have given us this much."

They moved away from the building and continued toward the docks.

Willowvine pulled away from the opening and groaned. "Now what?"

Springheart was gathering their belongings. "We need to beat them." He followed her to the back window where they leapt to the grass and raced down the alley. Willowvine knew they would beat the scree to their destination, but would it be enough?

At the wharf, she stood behind a bollard scanning the street for the Scree. They were in no hurry. Heads together, they seemed to be talking. Probably about how they will spend what they skimmed from the bribe money. She glanced one more time at the approaching scree and then raced to pass Spring-heart who was waiting behind another bollard farther down the wharf. There were ten well-placed hiding places between them and the first ship. They needed to be aboard before the scree arrived.

Playing a game of bollard leapfrog wasn't her idea of fun, but at least they had cover. By the time they arrived at the Land Ho, the first scree had boarded the ship closest to town, and the second one was strolling along the dock toward them, his gaze fixed on the end of the wharf. If they ran up the gangway, he could not possibly miss them.

Springheart tapped her shoulder and leaned in to whisper, "We'll wait until he's on board and then try to get passage on the ship behind. Not everyone likes dealing with scree. We might get lucky."

She nodded more in habit than agreement. Even if they could get passage on one of the later boats, they would be too far behind Maynard. The best choice was Land Ho, and she still had time to do the deal. "Give me the money," she said, holding out her hand.

He hesitated and she knew he was reluctant to let her go alone, but he gave her the pouch of coins they'd set aside for passage. It was twice what the captain would generally want, giving her a nice margin for a sweetener. "Can you distract him?"

Springheart nodded and removed one of the small knives he'd started using when they'd lived with Madeline. "You don't need to kill him," she whispered. A dead body would bring too much attention.

"I won't even hurt him. Ready?"

She slipped to the edge of the gangway, crouching in the sliver of the shadow left by the street lanterns. Springheart stood, flipped the knife to land with a thunk in the side of the ship that the scree was passing. At the sound, the scree whirled, looking for the threat. His attention distracted, Willowvine raced up the gangway. Springheart followed her closely.

On board, they crouched before the dozing sailor who was supposed to be on guard. Shouts from the wharf startled him awake. He looked down at them and said, "Oh, it's you. Captain is back. Told him you were looking for passage. Get down there and talk to him."

It couldn't be that easy, Willowvine thought. The scree had stopped shouting, so she figured he'd be on board in moments.

They met the captain, a younger man than she expected. Blond hair and beard, with a scar across his right cheek that pulled his smile into a grimace. She handed Springheart the money pouch. He was a better negotiator than she was. Then she stood back while he negotiated passage and paid the fee to the sound of boots striding up the gangway.

"We need to be discreet," he said placing more coins on the table in front of the captain. "It would be best if no one knew we are sailing with you."

The captain pocketed the coins. "Including the man who just came aboard?"

"A scree, and yes."

"Very well. I'll get rid of him, but then you need to go ashore. We'll be lading our cargo for the next two hours. You need to come aboard after that."

Willowvine didn't like the idea of being in town while Vitenkar was searching for them. "We can stay out of the way," she said. "It would be better if we can stay aboard."

"No," the captain said firmly. "Too dangerous. Go through there." He pointed to a curtain covering a doorway. "My quarters. We'll make sure it's safe for you to leave, but leave you must."

Chapter 33

As much as he wanted to rent a room and hide out until sailing, Springheart knew that a two-hour room rental would raise eyebrows. And he couldn't quite shake the feeling that Sailor's Haven was not safe since Maynard had hijacked the Stone. They were better off going back to the demolished house. Workers wouldn't be there until first light at the earliest.

They'd listened as the captain assured the scree that he would not give passage to an elf before hustling him off the ship. Now they were waiting in the shadows of a warehouse to make sure they could get back to their hiding place without being seen.

"Too bad that window is just an exit," Willowvine whispered. "The main road is too straight a line. They'll see us run."

The scree they'd dodged turned to enter the gangway of his last ship, the other was walking away from them.

"It has a slight bend as it goes uphill," Springheart said. "We'll be fine after that. Don't run. It will catch their attention. Keep to the shadows and don't look back."

Willowvine edged around the corner of the building and

strode confidently through the shadows along the storefronts. Springheart took one more look at the wharf before following her. They heard footsteps from ahead, not the stamping march of a scree, but not the sound of wares being sent to the boats either.

They turned the corner to see Devissial's servant walking toward them. The man caught sight of them and sped his steps.

"You are wanted," he said then promptly turned back the way he had come.

Waiting at Devissial's home would be better than the cold building, but Springheart couldn't help feel that he'd end up regretting following this man.

Willowvine tugged him back before Springheart had taken two steps. "Should I wait in the building? If something happens, one of us should be able to leave."

He motioned her on. "Nothing will happen. Devissial wants us to succeed."

When the servant showed them into the waiting room, Springheart started to worry. The relative security of the house could be a prison if Willowvine's concern was valid.

Devissial entered before Springheart could think through the problem. The man was in his nightclothes, red robe wrapped around him, slippers on his feet, but by the brightness in his eyes, he hadn't been asleep yet tonight.

"I have heard some disturbing rumors. I need to know what is happening so I can report to my contact before someone sends a message. If these rumors are true, then our mission is not as secret as we expected."

Willowvine sat on one of the sofas, clearly ready to be silent and let Springheart take whatever consequences were coming.

Truth was the only way to deal with rumor. "The Stone was taken from us and is on its way to the mainland," he said. Truth did not mean babbling on.

Devissial slumped, worry etching his face. "Your plan?"

"We have passage on the first ship out," Springheart said. "We will regain the Stone and sail from there to the final location in plenty of time to meet the deadline."

Devissial nodded. "You'll catch up time on the night sailing because it runs faster. You'll only be three hours behind when you get there. You clearly know who stole it."

It was a question not a statement, but Springheart was not going to give Devissial the power to deal with Maynard. "It's guild business," he said. If Devissial handled the betrayal, the guild would never know about Maynard's action — and they needed to know.

"If the guild does not deal with it, inform me. I will ensure justice is meted out. Does this person know what the Stone is?"

Now Springheart would have to lie. It would be disastrous for a client to learn that the guild room was not secure. "It is not clear. Since Willowvine and I are alive, they did not hear it from us. But we are not the only ones with the knowledge, so I cannot be sure." He considered what else he could offer, and then added, "Since the ship is headed to The City, I think we can be sure that the destination is still a secret."

The answer didn't make the man easy, but there was no other information.

"Very well. If you wish to wait here until sailing, I'll have my staff make you comfortable."

Springheart turned the offer down. The closer they could wait to the wharf, the better.

AN HOUR into the journey Maynard asked the captain for a bird to send a message. "To the guild," he said, assuming that every ship had sufficient birds trained to the guild.

It wouldn't be enough to just beat the elves to the Stone. It was certainly not enough to satisfy his plans. The elves had to be blamed for their mistake, and the guild needed information to act. By the time Maynard set his feet back on Lands Home, he would be the hero and the elves would be disgraced.

The captain gave him an assessing look. "We only have one for the guild. Ten coins."

He didn't have enough to send the message direct. The remaining coins needed to be saved for the journey to the elven lands. The general post would take a little longer, but not so much that the elves would avoid being called to report. "General post?"

"A bird is going in a few minutes. Two coins."

Maynard handed over the payment and scrawled his note.

The elves bungled the contract. I am continuing to fulfill it. Will return to the guild within days with details.

That should do it. The guild would have the message in time to prevent the elves from boarding any vessel leaving on the next tide. By the time they set sail, if they were allowed off island, he would be halfway to the elven lands. Halfway to being the best courier, and a step closer to becoming a guild board member.

Chapter 34

Outside Devissial's house, Springheart was relieved to see that the shadows had deepened. It would be easier to maneuver on the streets, which were now busier as the various suppliers made last-minute deliveries to the ships preparing to sail. The scree might be searching for them, or at least Willowvine, now they were supposedly trapped on the island.

"I'm not sure that Devissial trusts us to fix this," he said as he steered them to the side of the street while keeping alert for searchers. There was still more than an hour before they would be safe aboard Land Ho, a long time to wait, but probably not enough time to escape from capture.

"It won't matter," she said. "We will complete the contract and then he'll have no problem."

They arrived at Wharf Street, slipping around the final corner before Springheart shared his real worry. "If his contact, who must be an elf, hires others, it will get very hard to complete the contract."

"No one will be as good as us, or they wouldn't have come to orphans in the first place."

He couldn't quite feel as confident as Willowvine. He'd

lived too long and experienced too many problems to believe that they could stay at the top forever. But there was nothing he could do about it. Springheart decided to take a try at Willowvine's attitude. They were almost off island. In a couple of days, they would have the Stone and be on a ship to Crous.

"Halt!"

The shout came from behind them. Springheart's newfound optimism melted away.

At least it wasn't a scree, he thought as he turned. The man had come onto the street from the door of a cafe that was opening for the late tide trade.

It was the marshal. Guild business.

Willowvine was poised to run, but Springheart knew it would be better to face whatever the guild wanted, because they would never interfere with a contract. They may even provide them escort to the ship. Running would only waste time, and would likely drive them into any scree who were searching.

The marshal approached and took Springheart's arm. The gesture was worrying, the guild didn't go in for physical punishment, and usually just asked questions.

"You need to report," the marshal said, his voice low to avoid notice, but the anger was still evident.

Springheart jerked his arm free. "Very well, let's go." There was no point arguing. It would only take a few minutes, even if Maynard hadn't actually made the report he was supposed to do earlier.

"Should I stay on the job?" Willowvine asked.

If she stayed, at least one of them would make the sailing if his estimate of the purpose of the guild's summons was wrong. Of course, she had the scree on her trail. There was no guarantee that she would remain free, especially the way she took risks. "No. We stay together."

The short march to the guildhall felt too much like an

arrest for Springheart to feel comfortable. They were hustled through the private board member entrance. The guild wanted to keep this quiet from the other couriers.

Inside Lisseline and Deacon waited, seated behind the long table, faces grim, arms folded. They dismissed the marshal and when they were alone Lisseline did the talking. "We have been informed that you lost the object you were contracted to locate and deliver."

Springheart felt Willowvine stiffen beside him. He knew that she wanted to blurt out every act of betrayal that Maynard had committed. Springheart's goal was to give as little information as possible so they could leave. A full report could wait until the Stone was back in place. "Maynard is in possession of the object. We are aware of his location. He does not know the delivery point."

"Why does he have the object?" Lisseline asked, giving no indication of how they came to know about the theft.

Springheart considered what to say without seeming to lie. The truth seemed the best option, but just the high points. "He stole it. He was not supposed to know the details of the contract." He stopped speaking before he reminded them that they assigned Maynard. That would only get them on the defensive and there was no time for the argument that would come.

Lisseline's expression told Springheart that he didn't need to remind them. She glanced at the silent Deacon, then, turning back to Springheart, she asked, "Does the client know?" There was no hint as to her expectation. Having the client know a contract was going wrong was bad, having them find out from someone else would be worse.

"Yes, and he has confidence in our plan," Springheart reported.

Deacon finally joined the interrogation, "And your plan is?"

Springheart relaxed, if they were asking about the plan, they weren't going to interfere, or not interfere too much. "We know where Maynard is going. We are going to follow him, retrieve the object, and complete the contract. We are the only ones who have the information needed to do that."

The two board members held a whispered conversation. Willowvine nudged Springheart while they were ignored. "Why don't you tell them all of it?" she whispered.

He kept his eyes on the board members as he answered, "Think it through."

She huffed her annoyance but stepped back

Lisseline finished the discussion by putting her hand on Deacon's forearm and smiling. Turning back to Springheart, she said, "Very well. When you have completed the contract, we expect a full and detailed report. The board will need to deal with these events."

"We need something," Springheart said before she could dismiss them. Lisseline nodded for him to continue. "The object was originally stolen by a scree merchant. This merchant suspects that Willowvine was behind the recovery. We need to get to the wharf in a half hour to board a ship. It would be better if we didn't stand the risk of being seen."

Lisseline frowned. "I expect the reason Willowvine is a suspect to be part of the report." She scribbled on a sheet of paper. "Hand this to the marshal. You may wait in the hall until it is time to leave."

Taking the paper, he indicated to Willowvine she should leave. Reading the note, the last of his worry melted.

Ensure that they reach the ship. Springheart will provide the details.

WILLOWVINE WATCHED as the five couriers ran from the hall. Their job was to clear the path to the ship. If they saw scree, they were to misdirect them, otherwise, their presence made sure that she and Springheart had a fast and safe journey from the guildhall to the ship. As the last courier disappeared around the corner, Springheart told her to go.

Shifting her travel sack onto her shoulder, she matched his pace. A fast walk to avoid the suspicion that would be raised by a run. "So, when we put the…" a warning twinge in her chest reminded her that the oath was still active. There were people around, people who could overhear her words. "It, when we put it back—" The words were burning in her chest. The contract was going badly and if things went completely wrong, she didn't want Springheart thinking of her as mercenary. She didn't want him to remember her as a problem.

Springheart stopped her with a look. "I don't want to talk about it."

"No, I don't mean what you think I mean. Of course, the elves need us to… do this." She glanced ahead not comfortable with blind trust in their escorts.

"And you think they should pay for it," he said.

She noticed he was scanning the street as much as she was. Knowing if she tried to convince him to listen, he would keep arguing, she decided to blurt it out. "I'm sorry I keep causing trouble. I'm sorry I keep trying to get them to accept me when we both know they won't."

The wharf was in sight, and she could tell that the industry of lading ships was slowing. They would be safely aboard where they could relax, at least for a few hours. Springheart hadn't responded, and she gave up trying to make him understand. She could try again tomorrow.

One of the advance couriers slipped past them with a quiet, "All clear."

Springheart gave her a nudge to speed up. "You can't force yourself to give up what you want," he whispered.

She smiled and ran beside him up the gangway.

. . .

SPRINGHEART TOOK one more glance as they boarded the ship; there was no one watching. A sailor pointed them to a corner of the deck. "Stay there until we're underway."

He saw a few humans clustered together, and two goblins sitting on the deck smoking. They weren't the only passengers, so at least it wouldn't be a boring journey. Until they were away from the dock, and far enough to be sure they were truly on their way and not within range of a small boat to call them back, he would make sure they kept separate from the other passengers. After that, when they were safe, conversation would help pass the time.

Springheart motioned Willowvine to sit on the deck with her back against a water barrel, and then joined her. Still trying to believe that she was past her desire for revenge, Springheart said, "The elves will be grateful. They just don't show it the way you want."

She sighed. "I know. It would be nice to know why orphans are so hated, but maybe a bonus will come our way." She glanced at him, a sly shine to her eyes.

"I thought you'd given up your plans to punish them," he said, knowing it was too good to be true that she'd actually grown past the resentment.

Willowvine rolled her eyes. "You mistake revenge for good business practices."

He chuckled. "Well, you have time to figure out how to ask for the bonus without sounding like it's a ransom, or like you are renegotiating. The guild won't let you do that. We'd be jobless when they found out."

He realized letting go of such a deep bitterness was not like closing a door. It was more like peeling away the layers of pain. As long as she'd started on the journey, she would get there eventually. He couldn't deny, if only to himself, that knowing why the elves hated orphans would help.

"What about Maynard?" she asked, her voice barely audible over the bedlam of getting the ship ready.

Springheart hadn't thought much beyond taking the Stone away from the man. It would be tricky, but between the two of them, they would have the edge they needed. "He'll need to answer to the board."

"You think he'll just report back to them when we are done?"

Not likely.

"I think they will have to find him. We'll give them the report of everything he's done and leave it to the guild to decide." It didn't sound very satisfying, but Springheart only wanted to get back to their regular days of fulfilling contracts and living quietly.

Willowvine shifted her position to remove the travel sack from her shoulder. When she looked at him, there was a cynicism in her eyes that aged her even through her disguise as a human boy. "And if they let him get back to work?"

He thought it unlikely and said so.

She shrugged. "He's human and we're elves. There are no elves on the board. Humans stick together."

He couldn't argue with that. "His actions could cause the guild embarrassment, or worse. They will deal with it."

She shrugged and turned her attention to the activity on deck. "That's the problem. It means it is his word against ours."

What she didn't say still echoed in Springheart's mind because it was true.

Maynard's word would carry more weight. It wasn't right or fair, but a human would always come ahead of an elf.

Chapter 35

Vitenkar couldn't believe the report Ballian had just given. "How can there be no sign of them?" The girl had not done this alone. The other elf and the human were part of it. He knew that with every instinct. There was no way that an elf girl had outwitted full grown scree warriors.

Ballian straightened, cleared his throat, and said, "They must have been on the last ship on the early tide. They were away before we knew the girl was free."

Vitenkar knew that if his luck had been good, they would have found the girl before the first sailing. Part of him wanted to lash out and deny Ballian's assumption, but he knew that if his scree hadn't found a single elven child, then she wasn't to be found. He couldn't afford to look the fool in front of this warrior who always seemed to skate the line between intelligence and insolence.

As a merchant, Vitenkar knew to the moment when the tide turned, there was still time to deal with this. "How many ships still await the tide?"

"Five."

"Then find five of our warriors you can trust. Send one on

each ship. No matter the destination, we will have them caught by the time they dock." He threw another pouch of coins at Ballian. "Each is to search for the girl and her companions and send a bird when they find anything. Then they are to detain the criminals."

Vitenkar would go himself to catch them and retrieve his property. "And, Ballian, I expect you to choose warriors who are intelligent enough to carry out these orders."

Are there enough in my sorry excuse for an army to place one on each ship?

Ballian gave a quick nod and marched from the room. Vitenkar took pleasure from the obedience. It was about time his warriors started behaving like he was in charge.

SPRINGHEART PULLED the curtain that was their only privacy aside to see that their berth was a cupboard-sized space in the aft quarters. Two malodorous cushions on the floor were likely their bedding, but neither would be used. He would rather sleep on the dusty boards, and Willowvine was more fastidious than he was.

"We'll have to take turns guarding our belongings," he said as Willowvine stepped around him into the space.

"I'd rather keep my bags with me," she answered. "I'm not sure if I can stay in this room. If you can even call it that. I can feel the rocking of the water and we haven't even moved yet."

Springheart could feel the same sickening roll. Since it didn't help to remind himself that it was because he felt movement that his eyes didn't register, he felt it better not to share that with Willowvine. "Do you think you can manage until we are at sea? Then we can head up to the deck."

Willowvine nodded.

The sound of heavy boots running up the gangway and across the ship added a vibration to the rolling that only enhanced the feeling of sickness. Springheart noticed a greenish tinge to Willowvine's face. "Let me look first," he said glancing at the ladder they'd descended. "No one is looking for me."

She swallowed and nodded before settling on the rough planks as far into the berth as she could, invisible to the casual look. Springheart hurried to the top of the ladder, peeking above the level of the deck. A scree stood across from him, holding out coins to the captain.

"We have no berths left," the captain said.

The scree poured more coins into his hand. "I'll sleep on deck."

The captain looked at the pile of coins. From where he hid, it looked to Springheart to be close to three times what he'd paid for their passage.

Licking his lips, the captain held out his hand. "Settle at the prow. Don't cause me trouble. Leave the other passengers alone."

"Any elves on board?"

The captain closed his fingers around the coins, his hand testing their weight. "One male. Are you planning to cause me problems?"

Springheart could see that the captain was considering handing back the coins, but it was too much money to turn down.

The scree lifted a pack from the deck. There were as many bones woven into the fabric as there were in his multiple braids. "I said I wouldn't. Looking for a girl elf anyway." He strode toward the prow of the ship, only his first few steps steady. As the boat rose with the rushing tide, the scree reeled. Springheart hoped that seasickness would keep the scree from seeing through Willowvine's disguise.

The captain rose to stand beside Springheart's hiding place. Keeping his gaze ahead, he asked, "What story do you want us to tell? I may not be able to turn down this fortune, but I hate the scree."

Relieved at having an ally, Springheart said, "I'm a tutor escorting a human boy to an academy in the city."

The captain nodded and moved away.

A sailor cried out "Weigh ho." A rattling of chains was accompanied by bone shaking vibrations as the gangway was pulled aboard. Two quick thuds of sailors landing on deck after releasing the ropes holding the ship to the wharf were followed by a great rolling as they pulled away.

"I'm sorry but we'll have to stay below decks for the trip," Springheart said as he sank to join Willowvine on the plank floor.

"We should act like we're student and tutor," Willowvine whispered. "I can't stay down here the whole trip. It will get too hot during the day." Her tone was desperate.

Taking pity, he answered, "It's dangerous, but let's try when we are away from the island. Remember you can't speak. No one will believe your voice is a human boy's."

She groaned and closed her eyes. The ship rolled again as it turned toward the mainland.

Chapter 36

The swells smoothed out after a while and Willowvine's stomach started to believe it wasn't about to be dropped from a height. It gave her hope that, in the worst case, she could stay in the cubbyhole until they docked, and still be ready to find Maynard rather than recuperate. When they'd come to the island five years ago, they had spent the entire trip on deck, and she had been sick. Then she'd been ready to jump overboard to stop the nausea. Now, even as it eased, the occasional movement out of pattern brought the feeling back.

Springheart touched her shoulder dragging her attention back to him. "Let me check out what's happening on deck. I'll be right back."

Willowvine stood at the curtain waiting for him to release her. Standing helped. It was easier to adjust to the rolling.

True to his word, Springheart was back at her side after only moments. "The scree is sleeping. There are plenty of places to set our things down. Just don't draw attention to us."

She handed Springheart his pack and then followed him to the deck. Dawn was beginning to show the sea as more than a strip of light reflected from the moon. She was careful not to stumble as she followed Springheart to a space at the side of the ship facing the rising sun. Willowvine stared out over the expanse, remembering the earlier trip more clearly as the fresh air drove that last of the sickness from her body.

The view was somewhat dull, water in every direction. None of the islands were visible. The ship was moving faster than she remembered from before. She thought it must have something to do with the direction of the wind. The breeze tugged at her hood, threatening to reveal her hair. She drew the cords tighter, knowing that it would look odd for a boy to keep his head covered, but unable to do anything to disguise the platinum braid that betrayed her elven heritage. "Am I still a boy?" she whispered to Springheart.

"Yes, your face is still dirty enough," he answered quietly. "Make sure it stays that way until we are safely in The City."

She kept her eyes focused on the distance. A day and night of dirty face was easy. "Where is the scree?"

Springheart pointed toward the front of the ship. She saw the scree curled up around his sack. Braids splayed across his shoulders like a shawl. He was deeply asleep.

"It's not one of the ones who were searching for me."

Springheart shook his head. "Vitenkar had plenty of warriors to send. This won't be the only ship he has someone on board. Let's hope this one sleeps most of the trip." With one more glance in the scree's direction, Springheart lowered himself to the deck. "I'll sleep first. Wake me when you need rest."

She gave him both packs to soften the deck boards then settled her arms on the top of the railing to watch the waves, birds, and strange fish that jumped clear of the water as the ship passed.

. . .

HOURS LATER, Springheart was asleep and Willowvine didn't want to wake him. She didn't need rest and there was something more interesting to occupy her than dreams. The scree hadn't woken in all the time they had sailed. The sun was halfway to noon, she'd eaten some travel bread and drunk a cupful of the tepid water a sailor had offered. Now she wanted to find out what the scree was doing aboard ship.

In the last hour, he had turned in his sleep releasing his bag from his tight grip. If there was a message in there, they needed to know what it was.

She knew that it would be easy to search the bag if she had some privacy, but others were walking the deck. Their chatter might wake the scree at the wrong moment. If she delayed, the scree might wake and stay that way until the end of the voyage. Springheart would tell her to cultivate patience, but that didn't help when she itched to open the sack. What Springheart didn't know about in advance he couldn't talk her out of.

Another hour passed, the scree and Springheart slept as soundly as ever. A sailor moved from group to group, saying something. As he finished, that group would stop what they were doing and go below decks. He approached Willowvine and whispered, "The meal is being served. You can eat below."

She thanked him but didn't join the other passengers at the ladder. As she watched the sailor returned to his post next to the man at the wheel. He hadn't told the scree.

This was as close to private she would get. The two sailors were talking and focusing on steering the ship. If they didn't let the scree eat, surely, they would turn a blind eye to her activity — if they even noticed.

She checked Springheart. His breathing was regular. A glance toward the front of the ship showed the scree was still sleeping. Now he had rolled onto his back sprawling on the deck, his bag completely free of his grasp.

She shifted her weight, ready to creep over to take the bag.

A hand closed about her ankle. "Don't even think of it," Springheart muttered. "Let's go sample the cooking."

Chapter 37

After the meal, Willowvine started to move toward the ladder, but Springheart held her back. "We need some privacy," he said drawing her to their berth.

Had it taken him the whole meal to cool down enough to reprimand her? Willowvine knew she was doing the right thing. The more information they had the easier it would be to deal with the threat. Maybe the scree knew where Maynard was hiding out. Where he was heading.

Marshaling her reasons to try again, she watched Springheart as he drew the curtain across the opening. It was stifling below decks and she longed for the cool breeze of up top. Even with no shade it was better than this oven, and at least there the nausea was held at bay.

Springheart motioned for her to sit, then joined her. Sitting close enough to touch. It didn't help the heat, but they could talk quietly enough that no one could hear.

"I need you to sleep the rest of the journey," he said. "You've barely rested in the last two days. I need your mind clear so you don't take stupid risks."

She was far too wound up to sleep. "But we need to know what the scree is doing here."

"Right now, he's sleeping, and probably will for the rest of the journey. I spoke to the captain. They drugged him so he couldn't cause trouble."

That was even better. "If he's going to sleep the whole way, we can definitely check his belongings."

In the dim light, she saw Springheart frown. Was she missing something? If he would just tell her where she'd gone wrong it would be better. Despite the scree's slumber, the journey wasn't going to be forever, in fact, it felt like the ship was flying. They could dock early, and that would be good for catching up to Maynard, but bad if they were going to be competing with other searchers.

"I'm not tired," she said for lack of any real argument. Willowvine knew that she'd reached the stage of fatigue that felt exactly like alertness but was really just exhaustion. "I can sleep when we know more."

"The captain said you could take a dose of the same drug," Springheart offered. "In the right amount, you'll wake up refreshed. The scree is going to be befuddled for hours after we get to land."

The way he looked at her told Willowvine that she was being taught a lesson. Time to turn her mind way from actions and think deeper. It was always about getting caught, or it seemed that way.

"If I get caught then we have nowhere to run," she said after a few minutes of puzzling. "If we wait until we are on land, we will be dealing with a drug-addled scree and a crowded dock we can use to our advantage." She felt embarrassingly proud of her reasoning.

"So, I'm not objecting to the act," Springheart said, driving home the real lesson. "Just the timing. Now will you take the drug?"

She hated to trust her reason to a guess at the dose she needed. This would all be for nothing if she was dozy at the end of her nap. But there was a bigger risk if she collapsed from exhaustion. See, she could think things through.

"I'll take half. I think I just need help falling asleep. Can I sleep on the deck? It's bad enough that I have to keep this dirt on my face, I don't want to be covered in sleep sweat too."

Springheart took a small bottle from his pack. "This is the full dose. Take what you need. Let's find a corner where I can watch you and the scree."

THAT WAS NOT A PLEASANT TRIP, Maynard thought as he disembarked the small boat transporting the few passengers from the ship to the docks. Their passage had been difficult enough with the headwind making the seas choppy, but then a squall had attacked them, forcing everyone below decks to avoid being swept off the ship. He'd been lucky to avoid seasickness until he heard the evidence of others' experience. Then his nightmare had begun. What should have been a day's journey at most had taken almost two. Even worse, he had to face a return trip when he was finished finding an elf to take the damn Stone, and getting some kind of recognition that he'd beaten Springheart and Willowvine.

On firm ground he immediately felt health win the battle for his stomach. He was here and the elves were not. They were probably on their way, but he had at least three hours. In that time, he could easily set false trails, stock up for a journey, find a contact with the local elves, clean himself, and eat.

Clean and fed were the priorities. No one would work with him in this state. He smelled bad even to himself.

The side streets away from the docks were set up for passengers who needed the fast services that Maynard craved. Within an hour, he was clean, sitting at a table in new clothes, eating a fine meal. He really should come to the mainland more often. Perhaps when he was raised to be a board member, he would offer to liaise with The City. Surely there were ways of minimizing the discomfort of the passage.

Meal finished, he made arrangements to return for his laundered clothes in a few days. He needed little in the way of supplies. Once he was prepared, there would be time to set a few false trails before buying the information he needed to sell the Stone.

Next door to the washhouse was a travel supply store. The merchants here were far cleverer than those on Lands Home. Convenience for the customer seemed to be the rule. He dug a few coins out of the supply, noting with concern how little was left after the passage cost. But then, it only had to last until he could sell back the Stone. The elves would be generous. He smiled at the thought that they would have no choice in the matter.

Emerging a few minutes later with a travel sack that was ready stocked, Maynard added the bag containing the Stone to the rest of his supplies and made his way back to the docks. Only two tasks left before he could leave The City, and any followers, behind.

The bustle on the docks hadn't diminished in the time he was gone. There seemed to be a frantic aspect to the work. Maynard looked for a likely candidate to bribe into setting a false trail and saw a man sipping caf at an outside table. As he watched, two men consulted with the caf drinker before rushing off to follow orders, or advice.

Maynard sat at a table close by, ordered caf that he didn't want and started a conversation. "Busy today," he said noncommittally.

"Tide confusion we call it," the man answered, keeping his eyes on the frantic activity. "Don't happen often, but enough that we got a way of handling it."

Maynard watched for a few more minutes before asking, "What exactly is tide confusion?"

The man gave him a glance that was probably meant to express Maynard's stupidity for not knowing. "One tide slow sailing because of bad weather, the other tide fast because the weather clears. Hits us because we don't have regular dockings. Ships stay out there and expect to leave right away to time their next port." He pointed to the horizon where a line of ships was starting to turn away. "We got to get this stored to make room for the next load. See?" His arm shifted just to the right of the departing vessels.

Maynard saw a ship appear around the point of land that obscured the open water. His heart stopped and his voice trembled as he asked, "Where are they sailing from?"

The man shook his head at the ignorance of people. "Only place over there is Lands Home. That's the first ship on the night tide."

Maynard numbly thanked the man and left the table. There was nothing to be gained from staying on the docks. The priority was finding the closest family of elves before Springheart or Willowvine found him.

Chapter 38

Sleep had been the right choice, Willowvine thought as they stood waiting for the boat to take them to The City. She kept her hood tightly closed and her eyes cast down to avoid a slip at the last minute. The thought of a bath, or at least the opportunity to wash her face, shone brightly through the waning seasickness.

Springheart was behind her with most of their baggage, maintaining the fiction that he was escorting a student to school. There were two boats ready to take passengers away, and presumably bring new ones aboard. She managed to maneuver them onto the same one as the scree. Fingers itching to rummage through his bags, she sat behind him. He was definitely feeling the effects of the drug. Face pale through the normal sun darkened tone, eyes bloodshot, braids bunched from sleep, he leaned on the side of the boat and closed his eyes.

"Wait," Springheart breathed into her ear. "On the dock; I'll distract him. You just need to make sure he gets everything back before he notices."

Willowvine made no indication that she'd heard.

The docks started as a black wall. As their shuttle neared, it resolved into a complicated face of ladders, ropes, and pulleys. Soon she could see people hurrying along the edge preparing to receive whatever came off the boats. They would have a lot of cover for their plan.

Within moments their boat was tied up beside the wall, each passenger boosted onto the ladder to climb the few rungs to the top of the docks. The scree was the last one off the boat. By the time he planted his feet on the stones of the dock and placed his bags beside him, they were in the middle of a rush of activity as crates were tossed to the sailors below.

Willowvine watched as Springheart bumped the scree away from his bag, turning him around as he began a long complicated apology that was guaranteed to further befuddle the drug dozy man. She ran to crouch beside the bag, undoing the drawstring cord to see the contents. Clothes, a bag of coin, smaller than the one they had. A short sword, club, and some jewelry made of bones, feathers, and silver. No instructions to help them with their mission. Drawing the bag closed again, she glanced at Springheart who slowed his apology, ending just as she stepped away from the scree's belongings.

A flick of Springheart's fingers indicated the street she should take to meet him. There was a store on the corner and she pretended to window shop while Springheart made his way toward her. The scree stumbled toward the street that held his embassy. She smiled as she realized that he didn't even suspect they were in front of him.

Relieved that they had managed to avoid notice, Willowvine followed Springheart to their destination: a Mariai inn owned by Zerenia, a woman who had aided Madeline before her journey to the elven lands.

It was only a short walk to the cool of the shuttered lobby of the inn. Willowvine relaxed as they entered. Here she could be an elf. She loosened the strings holding her hood in place and freed her braid.

Springheart placed their bags on the floor beside the reception desk. "Is Zerenia in residence?" They had counted on her using her spies to find Maynard, and to distract the scree.

"It has been too long, Springheart." The voice came from the doorway of a small room off to the side of the lobby. Willowvine would never understand the need to tattoo your heritage on your face, but that was the Mariai way. Zerenia was small, and despite the numerous facial tattoos, she exuded elegance.

Beckoning them to her private quarters, Zerenia ordered refreshments and sent Willowvine into her private convenience to clean up. Leaving Springheart to relate the details of their mission while she was gone.

When Willowvine returned, feeling clean and more alert, Zerenia was pouring tea.

"How can I help?" the Mariai woman asked.

"We need to know where Maynard Slack has gone, and when, and we need the scree distracted." Springheart reached for their bag. "I am willing to offer a favor or coin in payment."

"Coin will do. I am owed far too many favors at this moment. Coin pays the bills faster. We will discuss how much when we are done," Zerenia said and then left the room to make arrangements.

"So, you think she's going to do a vision for us?" Willowvine asked.

Passing a plate of pastries to her, Springheart answered, "No, she will use her spies. We don't have the time for a vision. Eat. We may be on short rations after paying her fee."

A few minutes after leaving, Zerenia returned. "I have made a room available for you to use while we wait. Rest while you are there. I anticipate it will only be an hour or so before you have your information and we have the scree stumbling around in the wrong direction."

SPRINGHEART STOOD at the open windows to the back patio. He'd left Willowvine to unpack while he cleaned up. Now their possessions were on the bed in two piles, one that they definitely needed, and one that they could manage without. A few of the items in the first pile could be sold if they needed to raise funds, but he hoped they wouldn't need to waste time with that.

"Should we send a bird to the guild to let them know where we are?" she asked.

He turned at the sound of paper being folded. She was repacking what they would take. "We can't take the chance that it will be intercepted. The guild board only wants us to succeed. They don't care what problems we run into along the way."

It was good that she thought about the value of communication with the guild. They couldn't stay a team forever. Eventually they would take separate contracts, or more likely, they would part ways. He knew she thought him overly cautious, but it was important to survive a contract as well as to complete it. If she were developing a little caution, it would serve her well.

"When we start our own guild, I think it would be better to have regular reports. That way we won't have surprises when our couriers get into trouble."

He was about to remind her that he hadn't agreed to this new guild idea, when he was interrupted by a soft tap at the door.

A servant stood outside. "Bring your things, my mistress has the information you need."

Willowvine quickly stuffed their belongings into the packs, the sorting forgotten in her haste.

In Zerenia's room, they stood eager to get going as soon as the information was passed.

"You are fortunate," she said from her place at the table. "Your Maynard Slack left the city for a small village just to the east. It is called Hanstone. My sources believe he is waiting there to meet someone."

Their luck had changed. Springheart would take that as a good sign and maybe think more positively. After all, Willowvine was probably not the only one who needed to make some changes. He was in danger of becoming an old elf before his time. "And the scree?"

Zerenia laughed. "It is not difficult to raise barriers to anything the scree wish to accomplish. They would be better served making allies rather than displaying their strength. You will not be followed for several hours, if at all."

He drew out the coin pouch. "Will we need transportation to Hanstone?"

"It is an easy two hours' travel, perhaps less with your elven stamina."

"The cost?"

He was willing to pay without haggling. Zerenia would be fair unless she had changed radically from the woman he met only five years ago.

"You may need the coin. I will only take expenses now. You can pay me my fee later. Ten coins will be sufficient. Fifty later."

It was a costly fee, but the information was prompt and to their needs. He handed over the ten coins. As long as they didn't need to spend anything until they left, the remaining coins would pay their fare to Crous. They would have to work their passage back to Lands Home.

Chapter 39

"Do you think he's moving on, or staying?" Willowvine asked as they passed through the gates and headed over the sand toward Hanstone. She could feel success as though it was an aura. They would find Maynard, retrieve the Stone, and return it to the proper place as quickly as a boat could get them to Crous.

Raising their pace to a trot, Springheart answered, "I don't know, but he would be wise to find an agent rather than try to contact the elven council himself. Let's hope that this agent is meeting him in Hanstone."

"Wouldn't any elf help reclaim the Stone?"

Were her people so stuck in tradition that they would rather die than take help from a human?

"They would, but not willingly."

"That's crazy." She knew there was something she'd missed thinking about when Springheart simply glanced at her. He was determined to make her learn this lesson, to turn her into a thinker when she really was better at doing things and cleaning up any problems that came of her actions. The tactic had worked up to now, and she couldn't imagine a situation that they couldn't handle.

Jogging along beside him gave her nothing to do except think, and despite her preference for action she realized the puzzle had captured her imagination.

Her people were probably the first inhabitants of Cartref, the elven word for home, family, and security. They'd protected the world from invaders, welcomed the survivors and retreated farther into their territory as each new species found a place of their own. Now they were, if not hated, scorned by other peoples. Fear of their fighting skills reached into even the scree warrior heart.

"Is it pride?" she asked.

"Some of it is, at least in individuals. You saw how hard it was for the general to really thank Madeline and Jode. For all the invasions until the last, they never asked for help. Most people lost the knowledge of their arrival within a generation, certainly fast enough to be ignorant about the next invasion."

He faced forward again. Willowvine took that as her cue to return to her own thinking.

If it wasn't pride, there was one other emotion strong enough to explain everything. "Fear."

Springheart smiled.

Surprised that she had it right, she asked, "What could they fear so much that they would exile orphans and risk their future to stay in hiding?" Willowvine didn't look at her companion for an answer. Her question was to prompt her own thinking.

And what will happen to Cartref if the elves are gone?

She couldn't find a way to answer the question. At the thought of Cartref without elves, a hole seemed to open inside her. Something black like the being in the well between worlds grasped at her spirit. "We can't fail," she whispered. "We can't let the elves die out."

Springheart looked at her and came to a stop, reaching as though to catch her. "What happened? You are so white I can see your veins."

Willowvine bent at the waist to allow blood to reach her head. "I don't know." She explained the feeling that had filled her. "I think we are linked to Cartref, that our lives are the world's life. If we are gone, darkness will come."

He motioned for her to sit on the grass verge. They had left the desert behind them while she was lost in thought. "We can take a few minutes for you to recover. Has this happened before? Are you a seer? No, don't answer, rest. I will stop asking stupid questions."

She waited until the cold that had followed the darkness receded, and heat from the setting sun warmed life back into her body. Little sounds of birds and the breeze comforted her. "No. I don't think I can call prophecy. It felt as though the thought came from somewhere else."

From Cartref? No that was crazy.

When she felt strength fill her, Willowvine stood. "We need to get this done. At least some elves are brave enough to try to fix this. While we are outside the elven lands, we are not going to be obstructed by other elves, but I don't think we can rely on help from them either."

Springheart took a moment to ensure she was back to normal before setting a faster pace than before. "It is good that you have given up this revenge."

She chuckled. "I'm just willing to wait until the Stone is in its place. They still need to pay for the way they treat orphans. What on Cartref could they fear from us?"

Chapter 40

Maynard stood beside the open doorway of the abandoned barn. The fact that it was abandoned had made it the ideal hiding place, no door to break through, and no farmer to drop by unannounced. Unfortunately, the fact that it was abandoned also made it cold, uncomfortable, and dirty. Cobwebs filled the rafters, dangling down the supporting posts. No hay left to soften his bed, no livestock to warm the night air.

When he'd approached the village, the sun had not quite set. He'd stayed out of sight behind a copse of trees. The villagers had returned to their homes before the sun was gone, some coming from the two large buildings, and some obviously returning from farms or the smithy. No one was staying at the inn. He couldn't blame them. The tannery was not in sight of the village, but its reek made his throat burn.

When the streets were empty and the shutters closed, he crept along to the end of the village street, catching sight of the barn just as he decided that he would risk getting a little lost by continuing in the dark. Rest, even in this unwelcoming place, would let him move faster at dawn. The first elven village was supposed to be a day's walk due east. They would know what the Stone was about. If they didn't, he would tell them and then they would want it enough to pay well for it.

When his eyes adjusted, he explored the barn. The open area led to a set of facing stalls, too small for horses. There was a faint odor of goat. Behind that, there was a small room, a possibility of privacy, but it could turn into a trap if someone came looking. Other than that, there was the door to the paddock, which was jammed shut.

Above was an abandoned hayloft. The best use for that was as a roof to the bottom. The barn roof had collapsed long ago. Given his choices, Maynard took a front stall. It offered shelter from any wind, a measure of concealment, and he could escape over the low walls if need be. He recognized that the desire to have an exit was simply instinct. No one knew where he was. That thought gave him a shred of comfort as he rolled himself in his cape, the sack with his belongings and the Stone wrapped inside with him.

SOMETHING WOKE HIM. Wide awake and alert, Maynard kept his eyes closed as he listened. There were no sounds to give him a clue what woke him other than a light susurration of the breeze moving debris outside, the call of a night bird — hunting prey by the tenor. Those were all natural and would not have disturbed his peace. He gently drew in a breath through his mouth to taste any threats, only the taint of goat, and a memory of hay. Had he been woken by a bad dream? Like a frightened child? Impossible, he was not so weak as that.

Maynard knew that opening his eyes would end the possibility of feigning sleep, but his imagination was already filling in the demons. When he did open them, it was to fingers and an arm reaching to unwind his cloak. It was the elf girl.

She reacted to his gaze by striking for her target; his sack. Shocked Maynard couldn't do anything but react like an animal — attack. He sat up swinging his legs around to sweep hers away while increasing his grip on the Stone. She leapt up and avoided his ploy.

Once moving, he was able to think. Springheart would be near, prepared to attack.

Willowvine wasted no time trying again, this time her objective seemed to be rendering him harmless. She launched herself at him, trying to make him fall against the back wall of the barn. Maynard scrambled backward trying to anticipate her next move and locate her partner. If he had been less confident that he had made a clean escape from The City, he would have kept a knife free to defend himself. He cursed, but there was no time to pull the knife from his bag. His only advantage was that the girl didn't seem to want him dead. Incapacitated, but if dead were an option, they would have killed him before trying to take the Stone.

Springheart was still not in evidence, so Maynard focused on the danger he could see. Shuffling away from her attacks was not going to get him out of this. He couldn't hold the Stone and fight back. He couldn't drop the Stone, that's probably what Springheart was waiting for.

The girl rushed him again, and Maynard saw his chance. He was facing the stall opening. Rather than dodging her, he bent and rushed Willowvine, using his body as a ram. There was no way a frail elf would withstand the contact. As he knew she would, Willowvine leapt to avoid the collision, her feet running across his bent back.

There was no impediment in the open space, nothing between him and the street, a place he could run. Knowing the elves would be as reluctant as he was to alert the villagers, Maynard ran out of the barn, turning east. A short run to the trees would mean he had a better chance of losing the girl.

. . .

SPRINGHEART DODGED ASIDE to let Maynard run past him. Willowvine was aiming for the man's back, but he seemed to be blind to anything but the path in front of him.

Joining Willowvine in pursuing Maynard into the woods, he gave her the hand signal to circle around. Maynard was likely thinking he could hide from them in the trees, but that never worked with elves, and at night they had the advantage of being able to see clearly, unlike humans.

He watched her swerve to the right side of the still oblivious Maynard before running to the left. Springheart couldn't suppress a smile at how easily Maynard had been tricked into running directly to where they wanted him. By the way he was clutching that sack to his chest, it contained the Stone. It would be back in their possession in a few minutes. Plenty of time to question Maynard on his motives, and then find a place to tie him up until they were aboard ship.

Maynard glanced behind before entering the trees. It didn't seem to occur to him that anyone would come from the side. "How has he survived this long, let alone been so successful?" Springheart murmured, testing to see if Maynard was even listening for pursuit. The man didn't react.

Willowvine was supposed to get ahead of Maynard. They had worked out the best plan they could when they found him asleep in the barn. His snores had drawn them. Maynard really needed training in stealth. The first plan had simply been to take the Stone while he was sleeping. Simple, but they both thought unlikely given the way that Maynard was curled around the sack.

This was their plan B. Trap him in the trees, take the Stone, and run for a ship.

Within a few meters, Maynard came to a stop against the trunk of an ancient oak, breathing hard and scanning the woods as if suddenly aware that they might have set a trap.

Springheart stayed in the shadows of the neighboring trees,

waiting for Willowvine to show herself. A chattering call of a night bird gave him her position and startled Maynard. The sound had come from above. Searching the branches of the oak tree, Springheart saw a flash of elven hair. Was she planning to drop on Maynard like a spider? Too flashy, but there was nothing Springheart could do except watch and be ready to contain Maynard when she had the Stone.

Leaning slightly forward, ready to lunge, Springheart watched as Willowvine lowered herself down the rough trunk of the tree. She was silent; Maynard still looking around, less frantic but not calm enough to think to look up. How was she planning to relieve him of the sack? No longer clutched to his chest, it hung from his hand, but Maynard still held the bag like his life was contained in it.

As Maynard's breathing calmed, his body relaxed. They had fooled him into believing he had escaped. Good.

Willowvine halted her descent, assessing her next steps. She reached behind her to retrieve a small blade tucked into the back of her belt. Springheart knew that she wouldn't kill Maynard, but he was suddenly unsure how much damage she was willing to inflict. There was no doubt in his mind that she would want revenge for the trouble and delay the human had caused.

In a swift movement, she used the blade to pin Maynard to the tree through his jacket, dropped to the ground and wrested the sack from his grasp. The man had no time to react. She was running to Springheart's hiding place as Maynard started to reach across and pull the knife free.

Springheart ran forward to stop Maynard as he wiggled at the hilt of the knife. "Keep going. I'll catch up," he told Willowvine as they passed. He could get his answers while she made sure the Stone was safely on its way to the docks. "Get Zerenia to book our passage."

He didn't stop to check on her progress, trusting her to put the Stone's safety ahead of any other consideration. When Springheart reached Maynard, he swung and landed a punch to the man's temple stunning him. While Maynard's senses were muddled, Springheart pulled out the knife holding him to the tree and then swept the man's legs from under him. Springheart rolled Maynard onto his stomach and bound his hands before stepping back out of range of the kick Maynard mustered in defense.

"What in the name of all sense were you thinking?" Springheart demanded.

Maynard struggled to a sitting position. "That girl was taking too many risks. I needed to make sure that the contract got fulfilled."

A nice lie.

"You don't know what the contract calls for. Where were you headed with the Stone?"

"It's something elven. I assumed the elves would want it." Before Springheart could ask his next question, or even form it, Maynard glanced at something over Springheart's shoulder.

"Why would you think that?" Willowvine asked.

Springheart kept his eyes on Maynard as he said, "Did you not hear me? I said to run."

She stepped beside him, Maynard's empty sack hanging from her fingertips. The Stone was weighing down her own bag, which was slung across her shoulders in the manner of all couriers. "I did, but it occurred to me that he knows too much, and I had some questions. How do you know the elves will want it?"

Springheart knew the answer. "You were listening. Somehow you hid in the guild hall."

Maynard laughed, despite his restraints he seemed to think he was in control, as though he had knowledge they didn't. "Yes, and I know how the elves feel about orphans. Even if I don't know where you were to deliver the damn thing, I know the elves would prefer not to be in debt to you."

Springheart drew another length of rope from his pack. "You may be right about orphans, but no elf would feel indebted to us beyond the fee they paid to the guild." He tied Maynard's legs at the knees and ankles, and then retied his arms. "We will be going. When we are safely on our way, we will send a bird to the guild to tell them what happened and where you are."

Maynard looked around him at the darkness. "You would leave me here to the animals?"

Willowvine chuckled. "Whatever happens to you out here is on your head."

Maynard blanched.

Springheart felt a trace of pity. The man would be facing punishment from the guild. He didn't need to spend the night in unfounded terror. "I'm sure it won't be long before someone finds you, and there are no dangerous animals this close to the village."

Chapter 41

Springheart feared that Maynard would find a way to get free before they expected. He drove Willowvine at a full run on the journey back. They could rest on the ship to Crous. It was more important to catch the tide than it was to rest. Their time was short because of Maynard's side trip.

"I don't like the idea that we left Maynard that way," Willowvine said.

Springheart knew she didn't mean she pitied the man, but she wanted a more permanent solution. "We could have knocked him out, but you know that the guild board would hold that against us." He wasn't willing to think of a more drastic action, and couldn't believe she meant they should have killed him.

"There was a jail in the village. We could have convinced them to hold him until the guild paid to release him. Then we would know he was off our trail for long enough for us to finish the job."

They passed through the city gates before Springheart answered. She was getting better at thinking beyond the moment, but the complexities continued to slip past her. "Do you think I missed the fact they had a jail?"

She sighed. "So, you thought the delay was too much? Waking someone and bribing them?"

He nodded, glad that she knew what he thought, and hoping Willowvine would soon learn to think it through before questioning him. "And we don't have enough money for a bribe and passage. We may have to work our way back as it is," he added.

"You need to start telling me things instead of just expecting me to follow your lead." She dug in her pack as she spoke. "I didn't give him back his purse. It was mostly our money anyway."

He laughed, acknowledging her point. "You could have let me know you'd done that."

"It didn't seem like a good idea at the time." She hefted the small purse she pulled out. "There isn't much, but it's enough for a small bribe. And he couldn't have bought his freedom with only his charm."

As they stepped onto the promenade, Springheart was pleased to see that the docks were busy as usual. The hustle would provide them with cover. "I promise we'll talk more. Let's get passage and information before we run into any more problems. Your scree follower maybe looking for us again."

"I'll get some supplies." She handed him the purse after retrieving a few pennies. Willowvine grinned at his frown. "We need food. I'll just get a bit. I promise not to burn through our fortune — or get caught."

Springheart waited until she pulled her hood over her fair hair and wrapped a scarf to cover everything other than her eyes. "Be careful."

There were tables set up for booking passage. It was convenient, but too open for Springheart to feel comfortable. There was no option, though, and there were no scree in sight so it should be safe.

"When is the next ship to Crous?"

The man behind the table glanced up from his list. "How fast can you be ready?"

Not a straight answer, but Springheart had to trust there was a reason. He told himself that the feeling of an arrow pointed at his back was just a touch of paranoia. He resisted the urge to glance around to verify it. "My companion will be here in moments."

The man checked his list again then waved at a waiting shuttle crew. "The boats leave every quarter hour to board passengers. The next ship sails after this shuttle. An hour before another sailing."

This time he did look. Willowvine was approaching with a full paper sack. There were no archers aiming for them. There was a pair of scree stepping into the crowds of the market, but their focus was on the approaching shuttles.

"This sailing," he said. The man named a sum that would leave them with only a few pennies, but Springheart didn't want to bargain. They needed to be aboard the shuttle before someone recognized Willowvine. He handed the coins over, gave a shrill whistle to alert Willowvine to rush, and headed to the waiting ladder.

Within minutes they were below the level of the dock and the oars began to drive them toward their waiting ship.

MAYNARD SCANNED THE DOCKS. It had only taken him a short time to release the bonds the damn elves had confined him in. He was still too far behind them. No matter how fast he ran, only goblins could outrun elves. There was no sight of Willowvine or Springheart, or any elves for that matter. While they were rare, it was unusual not to see a few in a crowd this big.

He knew they had to take the Stone somewhere off the mainland. He guessed that it wasn't back to Lands Home, but it could be any of the other four islands. He had no money for passage, but perhaps he could offer courier services as trade. Striding toward the tables set out to sell passage, Maynard pushed aside the nagging doubt. He would find the elves and still be the one to complete the contract. Step one was to find out where they took the Stone.

It took three tables of rude men for Maynard to get the information he needed. Willowvine and Springheart had boarded a ship for Crous. "When is the next sailing?"

"You can board on any of the shuttles. The next ship goes in a half hour, then in an hour. They wait the tide at Crous." The man looked at Maynard expectantly.

"Who do I speak to regarding paying in trade?"

A roll of his eyes preceded the man's answer. "If they are taking trade you need to speak to the captain's representative." He pointed to a group of men talking and smoking in the shade of a canopy.

He had time.

As he strode to join the representatives, Maynard smoothed his clothes and pulled himself into a less frantic demeanor. He didn't have to rush at the first offer. Boarding a ship now, may mean waiting for the tide at Crous. His path took him across the line of passengers unloading from the latest ships from Lands Home. He nodded to a few people he recognized, none who he could ask to lend him money for passage.

At the end of the straggling line of people, he saw someone. Maynard stopped his progress and garnered a few grumbles as people had to swerve around him.

Vitenkar.

A new plan blossomed. He would create an alliance with

the scree, at least until they arrived on Crous to dock. He marched over to Vitenkar who had been joined by a second scree. The conversation was not going well, and he was surprised at the level of fear on the face of the second scree.

"Why did you not send a bird to advise me you hadn't found them?" Vitenkar snapped at the other scree.

Before the answer could come, Maynard said, "You are looking for two elves."

The two scree looked at him. "Who are you?"

Unconcerned at the sneer in the tone, Maynard said, "I know who they are, what they have, and where they are going." He wasn't sure how much the lesser scree knew and didn't want to alienate Vitenkar by revealing information that he would prefer to keep close.

Vitenkar dismissed the other scree. When they were alone, or as alone as they could be in the crowd on the dock, he asked, "What do you want for this information?"

Maynard wanted the Stone so he could continue to his goal. He knew Vitenkar had his own plans, plans that Maynard would deal with when they intercepted Springheart and Willowvine. "I want to come with you and help. I need you to pay for the passage to… our destination."

He could see that Vitenkar took his directness as a sign of weakness. Fine. It would put him off his guard.

A cold smile twisted the scree's mouth. "How do I know your information is good?"

"The fact that I know what they stole from you should be enough," Maynard said.

"What did they steal?" Vitenkar said the words they as though he didn't credit the information. As if they hadn't stolen anything of value. The scree was a fool and would be easy to deal with as soon as they arrived on Crous.

Realizing the man might not know about Springheart, having only caught Willowvine, he said, "Yes, they. The elven girl had a partner." He looked around and noticed that the crowd was giving them room. No one wanted to intrude on whatever business a scree was doing. Satisfied that no one was eavesdropping, he added, "A Stone. An elven Stone of Power."

Vitenkar took a step closer. "You will give me the information for the cost of passage?" It was part question, part threat.

"I want to be there when you take it back. To see them fail," he said. Then, thinking he needed more, he added, "I can get information that a scree cannot."

Vitenkar stared at him for a long moment. Maynard wanted to tell him to hurry, that they were falling farther behind with every second of delay, but he kept his mouth shut. Then Vitenkar waved for his servant — at least that's what Maynard thought the other scree was — and agreed to their partnership. "Do not speak of this to anyone other than me," he threatened.

Chapter 42

"That was almost two days wasted," Willowvine said as they disembarked. She looked around at the docks. This island was less populated than Lands Home, and less town-like.

The docks were just frontage with only a single street heading up an incline toward a small cluster of buildings. Two warehouses flanked the street, one abandoned and starting the process of crumbling to dirt. The other was in better shape, but by the dust and grime on the windows, it was only a few months away from the fate of its partner. "Does anyone live here?"

Springheart pulled her to the side to wait for the few other passengers to leave the area. "Yes, but they rely on the other islands to supply them. Artisans, poets, and scholars mostly — and their servants."

"And our contact," she added. "Do you know how to find him?"

Springheart checked to make sure they were alone and then drew her toward the abandoned building. "I'll just ask around. He's not hiding, or he isn't likely to be hiding. Someone will know of an elf named Leafcreek."

Inside the building was as decrepit as it was outside. Willowvine wondered what they were doing. Shouldn't they be finishing the contract, and getting the reward they deserved?

Springheart seemed to know what she was thinking because he answered the question as he wandered deeper into the dark corner. "We need to hide the Stone while we talk to the contact. We probably have a few hours before anyone else arrives, but we've already had it pulled out of our hands once. I'm not going to let it happen again."

"We have to get it in place tonight," she said pulling a few broken boards from a pile near the wall. "Here. Put it here and we'll pile the boards on top like they fell naturally."

He took the Stone from the bag and placed it next to a pile of rubble. "If our luck gets better, maybe it will be done before anyone finds out."

She snorted at the idea. Their luck was not likely to change until this job was over. They'd managed to lose all the leeway they had. Tonight, the Stone needed to be replaced, if it wasn't the contract didn't matter. Even so, she agreed that hiding it was the best move. It gave her time to negotiate the price.

WILLOWVINE HAD that look on her face, the one that usually preceded an argument. Springheart was sure that the topic on her mind was renegotiating the price. Knowing it would do more damage to the nonexistent relationship the orphans had with the other elves, he said. "This time we need to keep watch. I'll find our contact while you guard the Stone."

The look on her face confirmed his suspicion. Disappointment fought with annoyance for control. She didn't argue, which made him uneasy.

Looking around the ruined space, she nodded and pointed to a fallen beam. "I'll be behind that." She didn't wait for a response, just ran to the beam, leapt over it, and ducked out of sight.

He knew the argument would come later, but right now he needed to find Leafcreek and get the Stone back in place. Brushing at the dirt to hide the little evidence they'd left of their presence, he slipped through the open doorway and turned toward the cluster of buildings that comprised the village.

As he was about to run for the light pouring from the main building, Springheart heard voices coming from the docks. There should be no one down there. The captain had assured him that the next docking would not be for four hours. The crates destined for the residents had offloaded before the passengers, and they were the last ship for this tide. He stepped around the side of the building, caution overriding the certainty of the captain's words. There were two voices, and the speakers were coming closer.

"You said you could find the Stone," a familiar voice barked.

"I said that they were bound for here," Maynard answered. "It should be easy to find them."

How had Maynard followed so quickly? And why was he here with Vitenkar and another scree?

"This is true," Vitenkar responded. "Then why do I need you?"

They passed Springheart's hiding place and he listened as Maynard explained that he must report what happened on the island. "It will save you retribution from the guild."

"They cannot harm me," Vitenkar said. "When we are successful, the guild will have no choice but to stand aside while I carry out my plans."

Maynard's laugh carried across the growing distance. "You think you are invincible. That may eventually be true, but the guild is powerful and I'm telling you that you don't want to have them getting in your way. I can concoct a believable story, but only if I see what happens."

Springheart watched them until he felt safe enough to enter the building. Maynard and two scree were going to make this far more complicated than expected. A quick glance toward the water answered the question of how. A small boat was headed toward the place the ships were waiting for the tide to turn.

Inside the building, Springheart was pleased to see Willowvine still in her hiding place. No one else would have noticed the gray cloth hanging from the rafter. It looked like all the other shreds of detritus in the ruined room. To him, it was clearly a fold of her cloak left to hang as a signal.

It was safe to come in.

Too bad it wasn't safe to go out. They still had to find Leafcreek, but Willowvine needed to know about their unwelcome visitors.

He waited, knowing she would sense his presence and come out when it was safe. She appeared as he formed the thought, jumping to land next to the rubble. "That was fast."

He shook his head. "I didn't even get to the village."

She closed her eyes to focus on scanning for auras and held up her hand for him to wait. A second later her eyes opened. "Maynard. How?"

Springheart told her what he'd seen and heard. "It's going to be harder."

She grabbed his arm and drew him into the shadows. "They're coming."

The sound of approaching footsteps followed her words. There were only two sets, and they stopped outside the doorway. Maynard's voice cut across the dull silence. "They must be here, or in that building."

Springheart gestured for Willowvine to retrieve the Stone. It was no longer safe left here unattended. Maynard had found them too easily for Springheart to discount a tracking spell. The voices faded. If they were lucky, Maynard and the scree were going to search the other building leaving them a chance to run for the village. They would have to take care, but using the shadows was how they completed most jobs.

Leaning in to whisper to Willowvine, he said, "If we get separated, keep going to the village, find Leafcreek, and finish the job."

She glared at him, but there was no opportunity for her to argue. There was still no sound from outside.

"Can you sense them?" he asked.

"They are too close for me to tell. They might be outside on the street, or inside the building across from us." She glanced toward the street. "That's the only way out."

He shouldn't have been so cautious. If he hadn't decided to hide the Stone, they might have found their contact before Maynard and his new friends arrived.

"Be ready to run."

He led the way to the door, wishing that it was later and the shadows were larger. The sun was not yet set, but it was low enough that the other building darkened their side of the street. Once on the road to the village, there was little cover, but they couldn't take the chance of waiting for night to fall.

A fast glance outside showed the street was clear. The run to the village was going to take them a few minutes. They could easily outrun Maynard, but the scree would be faster, and it was too easy for him to call out for help.

He turned to Willowvine. "I'm going to go first. I'll draw any attention there is out there. You go when you think it's safe."

"Don't get killed," she said before stepping away.

He bent to pick up some brick fragments and then strode out into the street. It was clear, but it wouldn't stay that way. The way their luck was running, he couldn't leave it to fate determine when they noticed him, so he tossed the small pieces of brick against the closest window. It made a satisfying clatter. A shout followed it, and he heard boots running on the cobbles.

The scree rounded the corner of the building steps ahead of Maynard. "Elf, stay there and we will not damage you."

Springheart took a few steps backward, aiming for the open field beside the road. He would lead them away from the village.

He touched his bag, hoping they would take it as a sign he held the Stone. Both Maynard and the scree hurried to catch him, the scree's eyes alight with the excitement of the chase. Maynard a little slower, took the time to look around, probably suspicious that he couldn't see Willowvine.

Needing to keep their attention on him, Springheart darted toward the open field, pretending to stumble to give them hope. Maynard stopped looking around and joined the chase. Springheart made sure not to outpace his pursuers.

Chapter 43

Where was the girl? Maynard couldn't stop thinking that this chase was only a distraction. The problem was that he wasn't sure who had the Stone. He needed to take it back, and make sure Vitenkar didn't get his hands on it. There must be an elf on the island. It would be enough to hand it over to any elf — it had to be.

Vitenkar had spent most of the voyage bragging about his plans to dominate the world. He'd graciously offered Maynard an important position in the new order. That was not the way he wanted it. Maynard Slack would be no one's lackey.

The scree was almost on Springheart.

Maynard pushed his body harder. He couldn't let the scree get there first. Lungs bursting, he made headway, but just as he was about to reach them, Springheart veered and their path turned back to the buildings at the docks.

Maynard smiled. There was no place for Springheart to escape even at the water. He would have the Stone and the elves would be disgraced. He turned to parallel Springheart, anticipating his path. The scree pivoted and collapsed; his leg caught in a hole. Maynard heard the bone crack and kept running. The scree would have to wait.

Springheart was making his way back to the building.

Now Maynard realized his lack of speed was a benefit. He knew how to cut the elf off.

Keeping Springheart in sight, he ran toward the target rather than chasing the elf. Poised to change course if Springheart did, Maynard let himself feel confident. This was almost over. In moments, he would be the victor.

As they approached the building, Springheart turned again and ran straight for the docks. Maynard slowed. Was the elf going to jump into the water? Could elves swim well enough to carry something as heavy as the Stone and somehow escape?

The sun dropped below the line of hills, making it hard to see details. The docks and surrounding streets were dark, much darker than Maynard expected. Stars gave just enough light to see where Springheart was, but too little to show the obstacles in the way.

Maynard stood watching as the elf veered away from the edge of the dock and came to a stop. He faced Maynard, but was too far away to see his expression. It felt as though they were squaring off for a duel.

Relaxing, Maynard said, "Just give me the Stone. I'll make sure it gets delivered."

Springheart held out his hands to show they were empty. "I don't have it."

Footsteps sounded behind Maynard. He didn't need to look to know it was Vitenkar. Scree walked as though they were marching to battle, boot heels hitting the pavement like hard drum raps. He kept his attention on Springheart and asked, "Where is the girl?"

"Where is my warrior?" Vitenkar asked before Springheart could reply.

"He fell. If you think it's important, he is somewhere over there." Maynard waved his hand to encompass the entire right side of the island.

"He will keep," Vitenkar answered. "Do you have my Stone?"

"The Stone will be in its place soon," Springheart said.

Maynard turned to Vitenkar. "Don't you know where that is?"

The scree snorted. "What do you think I am? I did not steal it. I paid someone for it."

SPRINGHEART LET THEM ARGUE. He was only wasting time so that Willowvine could find Leafcreek. The more the two men facing him talked, the less energy he needed to expend. If he had to, he would jump into the water, but he preferred to get back to the building to make sure that Willowvine was gone. It just meant getting through Vitenkar and Maynard, a task that was not going to be easy.

The argument quieted, and Maynard asked again, "Where is the girl?"

"I don't know," Springheart answered. "Did she come with you?"

Vitenkar snarled and took a step forward. "We know she came with you. The other passengers at the inn told us there were two elves in the party." He turned to Maynard. "This elf is stalling. We need to return to the village. The girl will be there."

"I am not so sure of that," Maynard said. "These two are unpredictable."

Vitenkar reached for the hilt of his dagger. "True. We cannot leave him free. The girl will wait. It is a small village."

Before either of the men could act, Springheart rushed

them, trusting that his speed and agility along with their surprise would be enough to get him through to the street and inside the building. Once there, perhaps he could use something from the rubble as a weapon to even the odds in a fight.

Maynard stumbled back as Springheart shoved him with his elbow. Vitenkar was not so easily fooled. Even merchant scree were trained to fight. He drew the dagger and swiped at Springheart as he passed.

At first Springheart felt nothing. That lasted long enough for him to reach the dark interior of the building. It was empty. Willowvine had done as she agreed.

If he could get above them, in the rafters, the few that were still in place, it might save his life. Neither Maynard nor Vitenkar would waste time making sure he was dead, there was enough blood flowing that they would think him mortally wounded. Pain roared through the wound in his side as he tried to reach for a handhold. His knees buckled, and Springheart collapsed on the filthy floor of the building.

Footsteps crunched on the rubble stopping beside him.

"He is no longer a problem," Vitenkar said. "Come, the girl has the Stone and we must destroy it before she learns what to do with it."

Maynard took the time to kick Springheart in the ribs before following the scree out.

WILLOWVINE MADE HERSELF SMALLER. Springheart would kill her for waiting, but she couldn't leave knowing that he was facing two desperate people.

And, no matter what he would say to her, she was right to stay. He was hurt, and more badly than he'd admit.

Maynard and Vitenkar were out of sight, but she didn't move. The village was going to be difficult to navigate now that they were looking for her again, but she wasn't worried. It would be tricky, but she could dodge them. And Leafcreek would be looking out for them, not hiding. She wanted to see if Springheart needed help. If he did, that would take precedence and she wouldn't hand over the Stone until he was healed.

What she didn't have was time to dither. Springheart would be angry, but he needed to live in order to yell at her. Checking again that the way was clear, she darted around the corner and into the building.

Her eyes adjusted rapidly. She stared at Springheart curled on his side, blood smeared in the dirt beneath him. His aura was still strong. She had time. Stooping to touch his shoulder, she whispered, "How bad is it?"

He groaned and turned to face her. Eyes narrowed in a familiar annoyance, he said, "The Stone is back where it belongs?"

Taking heart that his voice was steady, she confessed that she hadn't followed through. "We both should go. You need help. I can't leave you here. They might come back."

He pushed himself up to sit on the dirt. "I have healed the wound enough to close it. The Stone is important. I'll survive until you finish the job."

Tears tightened her throat. "There's at least an hour until the moon is fully risen. We have time to heal you first. I'll make them."

Springheart grimaced with the effort of rising to his feet. "That same logic says I will survive an hour while the elves are saved. Even if I were going to die I am only one elf. You are risking the whole of our people."

She failed to suppress the sob that hurt her chest. "You've done more for me than all the other elves together. I won't let you die. And I promise I won't let the deadline pass."

He held his side and tried to shuffle away from where he'd collapsed. Willowvine propped him up with her shoulder. Logic told her they would never make the village with him so weak. Reluctantly she gave in. "Don't make it worse. Leafcreek should be looking for us. Stay here, I'll go find out what we need to do."

Springheart let her lower him to sit on a fallen beam. Leaving him hurt her, but she couldn't argue any longer.

Chapter 44

The village, if you could call it that, was a waste of time. Vitenkar was sure that the elf knew more than he was telling. He left Maynard to continue asking about the girl and made his way back to the abandoned building. The moon had risen enough to reflect sufficient light for him to make out shapes at his destination.

The girl was creeping along the edge of the path. Excellent. No need to argue with the human over the Stone. He would beat the girl until she told him where to find it and then destroy it, the only way to ensure the end of the elves.

The girl saw him and came to a stop. He hurried toward her, drawing his blade. If she was going to hesitate, he would take advantage.

As he drew close, she turned and ran for the abandoned building. Good two dead elves in one place would be easier to deal with than if they were scattered across the street. He could have Maynard bring the warrior here as well when they were done. Three dead bodies felt like an auspicious number.

He ran through the doorway, knife held ready to strike. The girl placed her sack on the ground and turned to face him.

A silver blade slashed at his eyes. He leaned back instinctively, feeling a braid fall as the girl's arm followed through. He swung his own knife as he leaned toward her again, but she danced away.

"You are going to make this interesting. Good. Tell me, is the Stone in that sack?"

She was too good a fighter to be distracted by the question. She flicked the blade in her hand, beckoning him forward. It was an old trick, and Vitenkar knew he was at a great advantage. His reach was so much longer than hers, all he needed to do was get the slightest edge and —

His thought was cut off as Willowvine attacked so quickly that she came under his guard, sliced at his ribs and was behind him before he could take advantage of the moment. He spun around, taking a rapid glance to make sure he didn't trip over the dead body of her partner. The lack of corpse registered at the same moment as the pain from a second slash across his face. She'd run past him again.

This wasn't a warrior's fight. He was stupid for thinking an elf would fight honorably. The cuts were a nuisance, but he couldn't take too many more. Changing his tactics, Vitenkar stormed toward the girl. Her speed would not save her against his size. If needed, he would crush her.

She skipped to the side to avoid him, but he'd anticipated the move and shifted his weight to follow her. Now she stood still. He was within inches of slicing her open.

Pain tore through his skull. He felt his knees buckle and then everything went black.

SPRINGHEART LOOKED DOWN at the unconscious scree. "He didn't even look for me. I thought scree knew how to fight." He dropped his weapon and pressed his hand on his wound. It may be healed on the outside, but he could feel the muscles tearing with each breath. "I'm not sure how much damage I did to him."

Willowvine took his arm and helped him to the fallen beam where he sat leaning against the wall.

"Rest for a minute. I think we need to move you to a less obvious place, so I don't worry someone will get killed when my back is turned."

He released his arm from her grip. "I'm fine. Go find Leafcreek."

She chuckled. "I wasn't thinking about you. I was worried that someone would come to see what the noise was about and get killed for surprising you."

"I don't have a repeat performance in me." He pulled away from the wall. "We don't have time to find a place to hide me. I'll be here when you get back." He waved his hands as if sweeping her out.

Springheart watched Willowvine retrieve the sack. Straightening, she said, "Unless the resting place for this Stone is across the island, we have time to make you safe. If it's that far away, then it's already too late."

Springheart sighed. It would be a relief when this was done and they could find another topic to argue about. "Willowvine, the elves are important to this world. Remember the knowledge we gained at the gate between worlds. As the first people of Cartref, we are tied to it. If the elves die out, the world may follow."

She firmed her lips against the argument he knew was bubbling inside. With a shake of her head she drew a length of rope from her sack. "I'll tie him up, and then I'll go."

Desperate for her to leave, Springheart reached for the rope. "I can restrain him. Go."

Tossing the rope to him, she spun and dashed out the door.

. . .

IF SHE HAD TO GO, then Willowvine swore the task would be completed as quickly as possible. The way everything got messed up, the elves were not going to be saved. She feared that it would be Springheart who died, not Vitenkar or Maynard, even though both of them deserved death. If the elves are so important, you would think the fates would conspire to help rather than hinder.

The moon had barely risen a degree higher in the time it took to beat Vitenkar. She smiled at the memory of how easy it had been to play his advantages against him.

There was no point in trying to sneak into the village. It took too much time and she could move fast enough to get there without notice, unless someone came out to the street right now. Her plan entailed circling the few buildings looking for sign of an elven house. If that wasn't successful, she'd start looking in windows.

There was no interruption in her dash to the shadow of the closest building. The village itself was a cluster of houses that faced the inn, like a caravan circling against foul weather. One of the small buildings had a healer mark on the door, another was clearly a shop. The rest were homes, fairly large, and similar enough to deny her the shortcut of identifying Leafcreek's home by the design.

She couldn't help glancing at the moon every few minutes as if time moved differently here, or perhaps her own sense of time was distorted. The moon was still on the rise, but the minutes were passing.

As she approached the inn, conversation came to her from open door. Two wide windows spilled light into the night. Willowvine approached the nearest, coming from the side to avoid announcing her presence. Inside, Maynard was tipping a mug of ale to get the last drops. He stood next to an eldmen and goblin. Others sat at tables in the rear, too far from the light for Willowvine to make them out. She would need to get Maynard out of there so she could enter.

As if she'd been granted a wish, Maynard placed his empty mug on the bar and tossed a coin beside it. Willowvine ducked into the shadows as he strolled out to the street. She watched him look around before turning to head toward the abandoned building.

"Waste of time," he muttered. "I'll get answers from Springheart, and then Vitenkar can search all he wants for the Stone. I'll have sold it to the old elf."

MAYNARD LEAPT the wall behind the building. His time at the inn hadn't been a total waste. One goblin, well into his cups, happily shared a story of looting the building before it was abandoned. The wall at the back hid a gap large enough for someone to enter without being seen. Apparently, the gap had grown bigger as the building deteriorated, but there was nothing to loot so no one had used it.

No matter how alert Springheart was, or how much he had recovered, he would never expect an attack to come from the wall behind him. Even if the elves knew about the hole, it was still preferable to marching in the front door and falling into a trap.

Behind the wall the space was barely enough to allow him to stand. There was no room for him to bend and search for the gap. He ran the toes of his boots along the bottom of the stones, gently searching for where the opening might be. Two feet to his left, Maynard's boot encountered air.

He explored the space in the same way. There was barely enough room for him to slide through. He didn't want to enter blindly, allowing his feet to go through and using the rough stones to control his fall, but it was the only way.

He had no time to worry about whether it was a good idea

or not. It was his only way in and if he didn't have the Stone to sell soon, he would not be able to repair the damage to the guild's reputation. No matter what tale he created, the blame would splatter over him. He closed his eyes for a moment to imagine the gratitude of the elves, the guild, and the world. Maynard Slack's name would be remembered. That thought was enough to silence the doubts.

In the back, the building was buried four feet or so into the dirt, so when he landed, it was behind a fallen beam on the ground floor. The noise of his arrival had him reaching for his blade anticipating an attack. None came.

In what had been the entranceway, Maynard saw Vitenkar lying on his belly, arms and legs trussed.

Springheart was looking at Maynard, a smile on his face. Everything about the elf read weakness. He was more pale than usual. His arm wrapped around his side where his tunic was stained with blood. It may have stopped flowing, but he'd lost enough to keep him from attacking. There was no reason for him to smile. He should be shaking with fear, but elves were all arrogant fools.

It would take moments to end both of these impediments. Then he would find the girl, and the Stone would be his.

VITENKAR WAS BIDING HIS TIME. The elf was weak. He would fall asleep soon, or simply pass out from lack of blood. It would be a moment's work to release the bonds, kill the elf, and then he could find the Stone.

The noise of debris falling turned his attention from plotting. Was it a bird or small animal disturbing the rubble? It took the elf's attention away and gave him a chance to act unobserved. Vitenkar worked the ropes on his hands against the bones threaded through his belt as he followed Springheart's gaze.

Maynard Slack.

Covered in dirt and grit, the man stood in the back of the building. "A rescue," he croaked through his dry throat. "Kill the elf."

Maynard took a few steps forward. "In good time," he said. "The elf is half dead. I need to attend to something else first."

As the man stepped forward, Vitenkar saw a flicker of movement in the darkness behind. This was too good. The girl was here. Maynard had not noticed, but he could easily take both of the elves and then they would be victorious.

"Behind you," he said trying to make the dry croak carry.

Maynard's smile grew wider and his hand flicked a blade through the air. It was poorly aimed if he intended Springheart to be the target. But the man must have not understood the threat that the girl represented.

As he tried once more to warn Maynard, Vitenkar felt a pain bite at his throat. He inhaled and something bubbled.

The pain tore wider.

He fought the urge to cough, and then hot blood soaked his shirt and the world started to fade.

Chapter 45

Willowvine watched the scree die. Maynard didn't know she was there, and that gave her an advantage, but she couldn't take her eyes away from the pool of blood. A sound broke her focus, Maynard had shouted as he advanced on Springheart, another knife in his hand.

Springheart wasn't strong enough to survive an attack. Willowvine dropped the Stone on the ground, a padding of dirt and rotten wood cushioning the fall.

"No! I have what you want!" Her challenge caught Maynard's attention. He turned away from his target and sped toward her.

She waited until he was almost on her before leaping to catch the beam she'd sat on earlier. Maynard stumbled past, scrambling to stop before he fell into the hole. When he looked up at her, she saw fire in his eyes, a cold fire. No passion, but greed and desperation shone from inside him.

She knew that Springheart was watching. She trusted him to stay out of the way unless he could deliver the final blow. She swung off the beam to land just out of arm's reach of Maynard. Keeping her eyes on his face, looking for the signal that he was getting ready to throw a knife, she reached behind for her own small blade.

Maynard stepped toward her changing his grip to a fighting position, he wanted this to be close and personal. She could use that.

He was within stabbing reach of her now, swinging his hand to slice at her face. She ran in toward the attack rather than swerve away.

The surprise of her move made Maynard stumble forward, allowing her to dodge behind and slice at his thigh. She wanted to cripple him, but her knife was too short to slice deep enough. Willowvine settled for twisting the blade to cause more pain and damage.

The wound slowed Maynard, but there was some madness driving him. He reached for her braid. Willowvine swung it away with a toss of her head. He was not going to get hold of her. The cut on his leg would eventually slow him down enough to allow them to bind him, but they didn't have time for eventually.

She ran around him and sliced at his arm, then dodged Springheart who held a length of wood in both hands.

As Maynard blindly followed Willowvine, Springheart swung at his head. The sound of wood connecting with skull echoed in her ears. Maynard collapsed mid-stride landing across Vitenkar's body.

"Kill him," Willowvine shouted.

Springheart looked at her. He was holding rope, ready to tie Maynard up. "No, he should face judgment."

Running to the back of the building, she retrieved the Stone. There was no point in arguing. Frustration tightened her voice as she responded, "He got out of the bonds last time, make sure he's secure."

It's not that she didn't trust Springheart, but he was weak so Willowvine checked that Maynard was secure before they left. The knot in her stomach didn't loosen after checking, so she used another length of rope to tie him with his back to a post.

"You healed him," she accused. "You are barely standing, and you used your life-force to heal Maynard." This night was never going to be over.

Springheart shrugged. "I only closed the wound to stop the bleeding. I'll be fine while you're gone."

With a kick at Maynard, she strode to where Springheart leaned against the wall. He was trying to look nonchalant, but she saw the pallor around his eyes, and the curve to his shoulders; he was exhausted.

"You are coming with me." He opened his mouth argue, but she held up her hand. "No. Every time we separate, something goes wrong. The moon will be fully up soon. We don't have time to fight off anyone else."

She watched the argument cross his mind. When had it become like this? They used to discuss things, now it was always a disagreement. Even though it seemed like she could feel the pull of the moon as it rose, she waited for him to answer.

He chuckled. "I don't have the strength to argue with you even if there's no one left to attack us. Let's go."

Chapter 46

The inn was warm as they entered. The quiet chatter raised Springheart's spirits almost like a healing. They hadn't made it as far as the bar to ask about Leafcreek before an elderly elf intercepted them.

"I think you are looking for me," he said uncharacteristically direct. "We have barely enough time. Do you have it?"

Willowvine nodded. "We should probably hand it over in a more private place."

Leafcreek took her arm and turned her around. "No. You must place it. Come."

He seemed to notice that Springheart was lagging behind. "Can you... No, I see you are badly weakened. I'll heal you more when we are at the labyrinth. It's not far."

As much as he wanted to tell Leafcreek that he didn't need any of the man's limited life force, Springheart knew he couldn't do anything more than stumble through a ceremony. "Thank you."

Springheart allowed Willowvine to support him as they crossed the space between the inn and the small house at the far side of the village. As they passed through the door, Springheart felt at home. There was something about this dwelling that declared it to be elven. The colors were natural, the fabrics were soft, and the furniture made of wood.

Leafcreek helped him to a chair. "Let me see the wound," he said pulling another chair to sit beside Springheart.

"We don't have time," Springheart said. He hated the weakness in his voice. "You and Willowvine go deal with the Stone. I promise not to die while I wait."

Leafcreek gestured for Springheart to move his clothes aside. "You are needed for the ceremony."

"Fine." Springheart raised his shirt not willing to waste any more of their precious time arguing. "Just enough to get the Stone in place."

"I know what to do," Leafcreek said chuckling.

The warmth of the older elf's energy flowed into Springheart. Too much in his opinion, but it came fast and then was cut off. He restored his clothing. "Where do we take the Stone?"

WILLOWVINE STOOD in Leafcreek's back garden watching as he moved aside a small cairn built of twigs, leaves, and feathers. When the construction was removed from the earth and placed on the flagstone patio, a labyrinth shimmered into being. She turned to Springheart who was standing behind her looking healthier than he had a few minutes ago. "It's small so I guess we didn't have to worry so much about time."

He smiled and nudged her forward. "Don't be sure. The ceremony might take a while."

Leafcreek beckoned them to the first stone of the path. "We walk the labyrinth and chant until we get to the center. We replace the Stone and then all is well."

Willowvine took the Stone from Leafcreek. "If it was obscured, how did someone steal it?"

Leafcreek touched her shoulder. "We have no time for questions. First the maiden," he instructed. Turning to tug at Springheart's arm he continued, "Then the explorer, and then the teacher, that is me."

Willowvine waited to hear the chant, willing to delay her answer until after the ceremony. Looking out over the labyrinth, she assessed that they would be done well before the moon was fully risen. It was small, as though meant for a child. The stones were laid out in three passes to a center space. It was far enough away that she couldn't see the details of the center in the silver light.

"We have only cast the concealment since the theft. In the ages that my family maintained the sacred maze, no one has ever been interested. Well, no one other than the elders of the elven families." As he spoke, Leafcreek moved Willowvine along the pavers making her stand on the second stone. "When we begin the chant, Willowvine will start, moving one step. Springheart, you will step onto the first stone and begin chanting. Keep a stone between you. I will then begin the chant when I step on the stone. The differences in timing will create a harmony that seats the Stone correctly."

Willowvine itched to get started.

If he doesn't stop fussing, we might be too late.

But then if Leafcreek felt no urgency, maybe he would answer more questions. "How did you know about the chant? Is it in an ancient form of elvish?"

"We created it when the Stone was lost," Leafcreek said. "The Stone was supposed to stay in place until the end of time."

Leafcreek's answers were plainly spoken, but there was no information in them. She was determined to get the full story of the Stones when they were done.

With a nod, Leafcreek came to the end of his preparations.

"The chant is six words; *Ethern Minalias ysgrd etoneth aluintail billianate*. They mean nothing, it is simply the sound we need. Speak them with the same cadence as I did and all will be well."

Willowvine ran the words in her mind to set them, then, at Leafcreek's signal she started to walk the path. As the others joined her, she felt the vibration of the harmony in her bones, then in her feet through the stones she paced. It seemed like the very air was shivering to their words.

Time disappeared.

The world disappeared.

The only thing she was aware of was her progress toward the center.

In moments, or hours, she was standing at the center of the labyrinth. She felt the other two draw next to her. When they were together, Leafcreek, still chanting, gestured for her to place the Stone at the top of a triangular indent. It felt as though the earth reached up to accept the Stone as she bent to place it.

The chanting stopped. The Stone sank a little, and the sounds that had enclosed them faded away. Willowvine noticed that the indentation would hold two other Stones, but the earth wasn't bare like it had been for the Stone of Family. Before she could ask, Leafcreek hustled them into the house with a promise of food and wine.

Chapter 47

Willowvine accepted the glass of wine and sank into a chair at Leafcreek's table. The ceremony had been short, but it had drained her energy as much as the fight with Vitenkar and Maynard. It had been too long since she was able to really rest.

There was still one worry to deal with. "We will have to go and get Maynard."

"Who is this Maynard?" Leafcreek asked. "A friend?"

Willowvine laughed, almost choking on the sip of wine she'd taken. Springheart explained the events that had kept them occupied so long. "We need to take Maynard with us when we go. I'm not sure what to do about the two scree."

Leafcreek placed a platter of food on the table. "This will do more to heal you than my magic. I will take care of the dead bodies. This human may benefit from the opportunity of meditating in an empty building. I will send someone to watch over him until morning. I hope you will accept my hospitality until you leave?"

It would be nice to have a bed to sleep in for the rest of the night. Willowvine looked at Springheart, he was better, but his face was still too pale for her happiness. "Thank you. I was hoping you would tell us the story of the labyrinth, and the empty places."

Leafcreek took a cloak from a peg. "Let me go make the arrangements and perhaps we can share stories."

When they were alone, Springheart said, "You didn't try to negotiate a reward."

He sounded proud of her, but she couldn't let him think she was changed. "There wasn't time. It just all happened. I'll settle for getting the story of the empty spaces. Do you think there are other Stones?"

Leafcreek bustled back into the room as she spoke. "Oh yes, there are two other Stones. But let us not get ahead of ourselves." He set them up with blankets and cleared space on the floor for them to sleep. "There is a way to tell a tale, and a way to simply give information. I prefer to tell a tale."

Willowvine started to urge him to get to the details, so used to being short of time that she was unable to let go of the pressure.

Springheart shook his head at her. "We can enjoy the story. We won't be racing for passage tomorrow."

She relented, but there was one question she could not put off. "Why are you being so kind to us? You know we are orphans, right?"

"I do not think of you the same way others of our people do. Let me tell the tale, and perhaps you will come to understand."

She nodded and pulled her blanket around her shoulders against a sudden chill.

"The labyrinth we walked was created so long ago that it has been forgotten by most of the elves. There were three Stones originally."

Springheart seemed willing to let Leafcreek tell things at his own pace, but Willowvine felt the pull to participate. "Is it like the one around the gate between worlds?"

Her question didn't upset Leafcreek. He simply nodded and continued, "Yes. The two have a connection, and there are only two before you ask. Well, that we know of at least. It is possible there are others. In both cases the labyrinths were built to mark the importance of the center. We are the first people of Cartref. Scholars argue about whether we were here from the beginning, or if we were the first to be drawn here. No matter, we are tied to the world. Our wellbeing is dependent on something in the dirt, air, and water of Cartref."

Her question still hung unanswered, but now Willowvine was drawn into the story and no other questions came in the pause Leafcreek gave her.

"The three Stones control the way the elves thrive. At least that is what it seems. The Stone we replaced is the Stone of Family. You know that, but perhaps you do not know its purpose. As long as it is in place, those with families will have children, not many but enough. The right-hand Stone was called the Stone of Abundance. We once had more children, many more, but few people remember seeing it. The left-hand Stone was the first to disappear." Leafcreek paused again to take a sip of wine.

Willowvine tensed. She knew that this next part was the answer to her question. Had orphans stolen the Stones? Looking at Springheart she saw he was alert and eager to hear the rest.

"That Stone was called the Stone of Orphans. No one knows who took it, and there was no request for ransom or reward. Some believe Cartref took the Stone back. That is why our people shun orphans. Either they believe Cartref itself has rejected you, or that you are an omen of the last Stone going."

Willowvine shivered from the chill in her blood. This was the stuff of prophecy, but knowing why didn't help her accept the treatment. "Is there a reason that two orphans had to rescue the Stone of Family?"

Leafcreek looked surprised at the question. "That was my requirement. I hoped that your involvement would help heal the rift. I am not sure it will, but I had to try."

Willowvine thought it was a faint hope, but it was nice to be in company with an elf who didn't make her feel as though she was dirty.

THE NEXT MORNING Springheart woke feeling stronger. Willowvine was chatting to Leafcreek in the kitchen. If she had known how weak he really was from the fight, she would not have been so cooperative last night.

He stretched and then rose. Folding his blanket, he listened to the conversation. It was inconsequential, like something that would happen between a girl and her grandfather. It bought home to him how much Willowvine missed being part of that feeling. It was something she could never have.

He joined them. "We should go and arrange for a ship."

Willowvine looked up from the soapy water and dishes. "How are we going to earn our passage and Maynard's?"

Leafcreek turned from putting dishes away. "You do not need to earn your passage. I will pay three fares."

Had Willowvine talked him into a reward? "The job was paid for," Springheart said.

"Yes, but this is my gift," Leafcreek said. "In fact, I will not give you the funds to purchase passage, I will pay for it directly. No argument."

Springheart figured there was plenty of room for argument. But the offer meant they could take Maynard to the guild board without having to pay for their passage with backbreaking work, and he wasn't going to turn that down. "Thank you."

A fast breakfast, and then they were on their way. Leafcreek promised to meet them at the docks after arranging passage.

Springheart and Willowvine strolled to the abandoned building where Maynard had spent the night.

A goblin was stationed at the doorway. "He is still alive, but he's not happy. Do you want me to knock him on the head?"

The goblin's eagerness told Springheart much about how Maynard had passed the time: railing against his fate, bargaining, insulting, and generally being unpleasant. "No. We can take care of him."

The goblin said farewell and hurried back to the village. Willowvine stooped beside Maynard and asked, "Are you going to behave?"

"If I don't, will you kill me?" Maynard didn't sound cowed. He clearly had a plan, or thought he did.

"No," Springheart said. "We are taking you home to face the guild. It's up to them to punish you."

He pulled Maynard to his feet, checked the bonds and then shoved him out to the street. Willowvine followed quietly. It worried Springheart that she wasn't arguing, or bargaining. In his experience, when she was silent, she was plotting something.

They arrived at the docks to find Leafcreek talking to a uniformed sailor. There was no ship in sight, but the small boat moored at the dock was clearly waiting to take them to their ship. They were leaving the way Vitenkar and Maynard had arrived. It felt good to avoid the inconvenience of timing the tide.

Chapter 48

It was no surprise to Springheart that the guild board hadn't welcomed them back joyfully.

The board preferred things to go smoothly and the complications that Maynard brought made that impossible. They had no one but themselves to blame for that. It didn't mean they apologized. In fact, there was definitely a hint of blame in their response.

On top of it, Willowvine insisted that they were not taking any contracts until she was satisfied that Springheart was healed.

Being idle for a week allowed them to observe Maynard's judgment. Springheart had watched Willowvine as the verdict was announced. As much as she pretended to be cynical, she'd truly believed that Maynard would be ejected from the guild. Instead he'd been demoted to the bottom of the ranks and stripped of his past successes. The punishment must have burned inside him, but he'd been given a chance to repair his reputation.

When he stalked out of the room, Maynard had turned to sneer at Willowvine, ignoring Springheart.

"I am not going to be defeated by a mere child," Maynard had said.

Willowvine had turned away and whispered, "I can see his aura. It's blazing with anger around a black core of fear."

While demotion wasn't a satisfying punishment, Springheart was sure that Maynard Slack was not going to be interfering with any contracts — least for a while.

NOW THEY WERE PREPARING for their first contract since returning. Willowvine lounged beside him in the shadows outside a residence in Wattren, a village across the island.

"We can go in through the window," he whispered pointing to the second floor. "The tree will give you a place to hide as well as a path up."

"It would be more fun to try the kitchen," she answered. "And it's closer to the office."

Springheart knew he would be wasting his breath to argue. She was probably joking anyway. "It's up to you. We have at least an hour before it's safe to try. I don't want to wait here though. We'll stiffen up."

She slipped away from the shadows and followed him to a cafe. "Why are we still working for the guild?" she asked starting a well-worn discussion. "I don't trust them to have our backs if something comes along."

Springheart waved for the waiter to bring caf and waited until they were served before answering. He used the time to find a new answer for her. "Maynard wanted to be part of the board. That will never happen now. The punishment was right for him."

She chuckled. "Never is a very long time."

He knew she was right. Maynard Slack would not give up his dream so easily. "We are still getting the higher paying contracts, but we don't have enough money to support ourselves."

He glanced at her and saw his mistake. She had a plan and he'd given her the opening she needed.

"Did you see what happened to Vitenkar's business?" she asked.

Wondering how this related to her plan, Springheart waited. Vitenkar's body had appeared a few days after they returned. Someone found a way to place it in the courtyard of the scree's home, along with the body of his warrior. Overnight the mercenaries disappeared. One of his lieutenants was managing the business, ostensibly until family was found to take over. There didn't seem to be much of a search going on.

"I guess we're safe from retribution from them, at least," she said.

What was stopping Willowvine from just telling him her plan? Had she suddenly learned caution? "Whoever delivered the bodies made it look like they killed each other, so yes, we won't be facing a blood revenge."

Willowvine took in a deep breath then sat forward. "I think we should go find the other Stones." The words came out a rush and now she held her breath waiting for him to respond.

It had been on his mind since Leafcreek told them the history. "How will we fund this search?" That was the first of a series of questions he'd been trying to answer and he hoped her plan would settle it.

"I think Leafcreek would help," she said eyes shining with hope. "And maybe there are other elves like him."

Springheart wasn't sure it would work, but there were few other options since the blood oath might prevent them from asking questions of anyone else. He would visit Devissial when they returned to have him release them from the oath. "Where would we start looking?"

A grin lit her face. She knew that he was agreeing, at least in principle. "I don't know. But we can worry about that if we get support. Maybe we'll be able to find someone to help, maybe Leafcreek has a clue? Maybe we can get Zerenia to give us a vision."

It was going to happen. He knew that as soon as he saw the empty spaces at the center of the labyrinth. "We need to get this job done before we even start planning."

He tossed a few coins on the table and started walking to the house they needed to burgle so that they could start on their new job.

Saving the elves — again.

Want More?

If you enjoyed reading The Elven Stones: Family, please consider helping other readers to find the story by leaving a review.

Must all the Elven Stones be restored before Willowvine finds acceptance with her people? Use the QR code to grab your copy of The Elven Stones: Abundance today.

Sneak peek ahead.

Chapter 1

Leafcreek poured boiling water over the tea leaves as he tried to digest the news. He was old, even for an elf, but he wasn't ready to leave the world just yet. The Elven Stones needed protecting and, he hoped, the missing ones replaced. When the two young elves, Springheart and Willowvine, found the Stone of Family last year he hadn't expected them to agree to find the other two Stones.

Last year, he'd had time. The quest to find the Stones should take years of planning and research, but now that would have to change. Finding a replacement for his role as Guardian was more important than finding the missing Stones. He should have done that long ago, when it became clear that his own child was not going to follow him in the role. He felt a chill run through his body at the fear he wouldn't have time to choose his successor. That some elf would be appointed, one who didn't know the nuances of caring for the future.

Shame followed the fear. A constant companion since the Stones had disappeared during his family's watch. Not Leafcreek's own watch. The Stone of Abundance had disappeared one night during his grandfather's watch. The Stone of Orphan had been gone for generations before that.

Leafcreek knew that some of the younger elves, those in their early hundreds, didn't believe that the Stones were vital to the elves' survival. That their small number of children was a natural evolution. Even those doubters disdained orphans. Leafcreek knew that the disappearance of the Orphan Stone had initiated the exile of orphans. They were deemed bad luck because of the loss.

Somehow these Stones tied the world of Cartref to the fate of the elves. They were the original species. The others, the humans, the fay, the scree, and all the different people were brought through the Well At The Center Of The World. A portal between universes; one that was closed by the human woman Madeline.

"I think the tea is ready," Heartfern, the healer, said, pulling Leafcreek from his thoughts. "The news has upset you. I am sorry to have brought it to your door."

Leafcreek smiled as he reached for the honey jar. "Not at all. A healer often bears unwelcome news." He turned and caught Heartfern's concerned expression just before the elf controlled it. It was a surprise, but perhaps it shouldn't be. Heartfern was younger than Leafcreek, but not by so much. He still managed to stand tall, where Leafcreek knew he stooped with the years. They both had brightness in their eyes, Leafcreek's still dark blue but would fade in the last few days of his life. Heartfern still had a full head of white-blond hair, while Leafcreek's own was more white than blond these days.

Taking the offered mug of tea, Heartfern said, "All is not bad. At least we elves do not wither away like others. You will feel your energy waning a little, please try not to overexert yourself."

"I will try to follow that advice, my friend. But no matter what I do, I have a mere six months to finish my life's work."

He didn't confess that his work would likely drain his energy. Leafcreek would gladly give some of those months to ensure he trained a replacement, and that three Stones sat at the center of his labyrinth before he closed his eyes for the last time.

"This is true."

Leafcreek could feel Heartfern's healer power as the other elf scrutinized his reactions. "Do not worry, Heartfern. I am not going to drop dead under your gaze. I will live for as much time as I am given."

"I can postpone my sailing. I can stay for a few more days."

Leafcreek needed contemplation time, not comfort or care. "Surely your other patients need you? I cannot ask you to stay on this small island any longer than necessary." He finished his tea and waited for Heartfern to agree to go. He attempted to look healthy. "Your ship sails in an hour if I remember correctly."

He could see the struggle on Heartfern's face. Elves were rarely emotional, but this man was not just a healer, he was a long-time friend. Leafcreek knew that the pull of grief was adding to the pain of a healer who couldn't do anything for his patient.

"I would not be missed so much for a few days," he said. "You may regret being alone. Even if it is just to visit with you, I feel I should stay."

Leafcreek found himself envious of the humans and other beings who could be direct in their communications. He wanted Heartfern on the ship, on his way back to the mainland. There were messages to send, and his home was a day away from the people who could help, even as a bird travels.

"Heartfern, you act as though this news is a surprise; no, a shock. Do you not believe that I've known my time was coming? I am old. Very old even for one of our kind."

"That does not make a difference to some people. I have had patients older than you who were completely taken aback to find they were not immortal. It is one thing to know you are old, and another to know your life is ending."

Leafcreek smiled in acknowledgment of the sentiment. "Perhaps I am denying the inevitable, old friend. But I know that I have too much to do in this last six months of a very long and eventful life. I promise you that I will reach for your help if I find myself in need. But I will not be alone for long. I must find a new Guardian for the Stones, and perhaps I will be lucky to find one who is more successful than my family has been. Perhaps that is why I am the last of my family to take the role of Guardian. Perhaps we have outlived our ability to keep the Stones safe."

"Oh, I think you have done well. There may be two missing, but you have protected the important one." Heartfern handed his empty mug to Leafcreek and bent to pick up his travel bag. "I will do as you wish."

Leafcreek took his cloak from the peg. It was chilly out this early and he wanted to make sure Heartfern boarded his boat. It was no use responding to the comment about the Stones. When all of them were replaced, someone else would take on the task of convincing his people that abundant children and the acceptance of the orphans was a good thing for all elves.

Chapter 2

A few hours later, Leafcreek sat in his garden looking out over the smooth, worn rocks of the labyrinth that led to the circle of grass that should hold the three Stones of power. To a stranger, the view was of a lawn bordered by flower beds and herbs. Only those that the Guardian allowed could see the path. This wasn't always so, but when the Scree merchant had taken the Stone of Family, Leafcreek applied the concealment.

He sat waiting for the peace he needed to compose the message to Springheart and Willowvine. The two elves had retrieved the Stone of Family and replaced it. Leafcreek knew from their participation in that ceremony that neither of them was a candidate for his replacement as Guardian. They had other quests in their future.

His request to them needed to be urgent enough for them to come immediately, but they could not know of his looming death. Leafcreek wasn't usually one to pay attention to his fears, but whenever he thought of Heartfern's words, his body tensed as though readying for an attack. It could be that his friend was correct, and the knowledge that his life was ending was overwhelming him, but it could also be a warning, a prophecy that couldn't be ignored.

The soonest anyone could arrive, was two days. The trip from the mainland or from Lands Home, where Springheart and Willowvine lived, was a day. And he couldn't expect anyone to take the message and run to the nearest ship.

The message could not mention the details of the quest either. If it were to be intercepted, it would not bode well. The Scree who stole the Stone of Family was dead, but there were others who would gladly see the elves wither away to nothing. Few people outside the elven scholars and himself knew that there was some mysterious link between the planet and the elves.

In the silence, Leafcreek felt the pull of the Stones. Even though two were absent, he felt their presence. It was like the pain of a lost love. If only it gave a hint as to the direction that Springheart and Willowvine should take, it would be of use. As it was, the pull was plaintive and directionless.

He took a sheet of parchment and composed the letter that would be carried by a bird to the courier's guild on Lands Home. With luck, the two elves would receive it by tomorrow evening.

My friends, he wrote.

It would be a pleasure to see you in my home again soon. I feel that the time is getting close for us to take the second step in the journey we began last year. If you are able to join me, I would welcome you joyfully.

That should be clear enough about the purpose. Now how to impart the urgency.

He looked down at the two message birds in the small cage beside him. He'd picked them up from the post office this morning on his way back from the docks. When the message was done, he simply had to insert it into the small leather tube and attach it to the bird's leg. The first would head to Lands Home, the second to his friend on the mainland.

Leafcreek felt no warning pains when he thought about his search for a replacement. An urgency, yes, but nothing that made him wary of sharing that.

I must advise you that I can accommodate your visit in my home for the next week, but after that, I will have other visitors. I am beginning my search for a successor, finally. It is a shame I have left it until this late date.

Please let me know if you can join me.

With wishes for your fortune,

Leafcreek.

He placed a few pebbles on the corners of the parchment to let the ink dry. While he waited, Leafcreek decided to walk the labyrinth for contemplation. He stood at the first stepping stone and cleared his thoughts. When he felt calm, he moved from stone to stone enjoying the heat of the sun transferring to his bare feet, leaving behind his cares and fears about the future. Coming to the realization at the center of the pattern that he couldn't worry about the future of the elves or the world. His job before he died was to find a new Guardian and at least start the process of returning the Power Stones to their place.

During the walk out of the labyrinth, joy filled him. He knew he could trust Springheart and Willowvine to complete the tasks. He believed that his friend on the mainland would find good candidates for his replacement.

Returning to the table, he tested the ink. It was dry. Leafcreek rolled the parchment and inserted it into the tube. He reached into the cage and selected the bird for Lands Home, the one with the red feathers on its breast, and bade it to carry his message.

The bird flew upward and then headed west. Leafcreek's fears crashed through the peace he'd found. Lands Home was due east.

Before he could recall it with a whistle, the bird soared

higher and then seemed to find its bearings. Taking a tight spiral, it dropped lower and turned to the east.

MUST ALL the Elven Stones be restored before Willowvine finds acceptance with her people? Use the QR code to grab your copy of The Elven Stones: Abundance today.

Free ebook

Claim your copy of Obstacles of Magic when you use the QR code to sign up for my newsletter and learn more about Madeline's history with magic.

Also by P A Wilson

For more books by P A Wilson

Use the QR code below or go to pawilson.ca

About the Author

Perry Wilson is a Canadian author based in Vancouver, BC who has big ideas and an itch to tell stories. Having spent some time on university, a career, and life in general, she returned to writing in 2008 and hasn't looked back since (well, maybe a little, but only while parallel parking).

She is a member of the Vancouver Writers Social Group, The Royal City Literary Arts Society, and The Surrey Writing Workshop. Perry has self-published several novels. She writes the Madeline Journeys, a fantasy series about a high-powered lawyer who finds herself trapped in a magical world, the Quinn Larson Quests, which follows the adventures of a wizard named Quinn who must contend with volatile fae in the heart of Vancouver, and the Charity Deacon Investigations, a mystery thriller series about a private eye who tends to fall into serious trouble with her cases, and The Riverton Romances, a series based in a small town in Oregon, one of her favorite states. Her stand-alone novels are Breaking the Bonds, Closing the Circle, and The Dragon at The Edge of The Map.

For more information
www.pawilson.ca
pawilson@pawilson.ca

Acknowledgments

People think that the process of writing is solitary. That's not the case for me. I have help from so many people it would be hard to acknowledge everyone, but I'll give it a try.

The support and inspiration I get from my writer's groups is incalculable. The Vancouver Writers Social Group opens my mind to other ways of telling a story. The Royal City Literary Arts Society gives me the opportunity to meet and share with other writers who have more knowledge than I do. The Other 11 Months group is where I learn about getting the words on the page. And my critique group who helps me find the best parts of the story I want to tell. Thanks to all of the members of these great groups.

Last of all, but definitely a huge part of the process, my beta readers. These are the people who love stories and are willing, and more than able, to tell me if my finished story is ready for you, my readers.